Dingo: The Dog who Conquered a Continent

# Dingo: The Dog who Conquered a Continent

## Jackie French

Angus&Robertson
An imprint of HarperCollins*Children'sBooks*

**Angus&Robertson**
An imprint of HarperCollins*Children'sBooks*, Australia

First published in Australia in 2012
by HarperCollins*Publishers* Australia Pty Limited
ABN 36 009 913 517
harpercollins.com.au



**HarperCollins*Publishers***
Level 13, 201 Elizabeth Street, Sydney NSW 2000, Australia
Unit D1, 63 Apollo Drive, Rosedale, Auckland 0632, New Zealand
A 53, Sector 57, Noida, UP, India
1 London Bridge Street, London SE1 9GF, United Kingdom
2 Bloor Street East, 20th floor, Toronto, Ontario M4W 1A8, Canada
195 Broadway, New York NY 10007, USA

National Library of Australia Cataloguing-in-Publication entry:

French, Jackie.
Dingo : the dog who conquered a continent / Jackie French.
ISBN: 978 0 7322 9311 6 (pbk.)
Animal stars ; 6.
For primary school age.
Dingo — Juvenile fiction.
A823.4

Cover design by Natalie Winter
Cover images: two men and a dog in a canoe by Oliver Strewe / Getty Images; boy aiming bow and arrow by Gavriel Jecan / Getty Images; all other images by shutterstock.com
Typeset in Bookman 10/14pt by Kirby Jones
Printed and bound in Australia by McPherson's Printing Group
The papers used by HarperCollins in the manufacture of this book are a natural, recyclable product made from wood grown in sustainable plantation forests. The fibre source and manufacturing processes meet recognised international environmental standards, and carry certification.

*To Hank Huffington,*
*with love and gratitude*
*for your inspiration*

CHAPTER 1

# The Dog

*An island in the great ocean, the Dry Season*

It was a bad day to be a rubbish dog.

The dog cowered as the bony boy threw another rock at her. Humans threw stones, but there were scraps around their camps.

She peered out from behind a tree, waiting till the bony boy was busy checking his spears in the grey dawn light with the other hunters.

The dog slunk back to the pile of shark heads. Her brothers and sisters and a couple of uncle dogs pulled at the sharkskin. There wasn't much left. The dog hoped the hunters would bring back more meat or fish soon.

The rubbish dog began to eat too, but cautiously.

The soft light before the dawn was usually a good time to raid the camp's rubbish heaps. But this dawn the whole camp was busy, women yawning as they slung their babies on their backs and checked their carry bags, the men oiling their spears.

Over near by the lagoon men dug a pit and boys dragged driftwood into a pile.

The dog sniffed the air. Change meant danger, she thought, as the hunters jogged past into the trees. The bony boy bent down and picked up another rock.

The dog slunk down on her tummy behind the pile of shark heads.

This was not a good day to be a dog.

CHAPTER 2

# Loa

Loa smiled grimly as his rock hit the rubbish dog. He hated dogs. He hated everything today.

Loa ran to catch up with the other hunters. Above the jungle the dawn grey swallowed the stars.

This was the worst day of all his thirteen years.

It should have been the best. Only a few months ago he'd been a boy, watching enviously as the hunters left the camp while he gathered tubers and shellfish with the women.

But today he was a man. Today he hunted pig, the most dangerous hunt of all. A boar's tusks could kill a man. You needed many hunters to catch a pig, needed spears and nets.

His spear was good. His father had helped straighten the wood in hot wet sand, so it would fly straight and hit hard. His grandfather had struck the rock to make the spearhead, showing him how to break off the stone flake by flake until you were left with a sharp, sturdy point.

Like the older hunters, Loa wore leaves tucked into the string about his waist. Pigs were clever. They were wary of a man-shaped shadow. A good hunter disguised his shape, stood with his legs together so his shadow looked like a tree's. A good hunter knew how to place his feet softly on the earth.

Loa glanced at his father and grandfather, jogging at the front of the pack of hunters, looking for pig tracks. His grandfather was the best pig hunter in the world! He'd taught Loa well.

They'd find a pig today.

For Leki's wedding feast.

Leki! Loa's heart clenched. He and Leki had played together as babies in the sand by the lagoon, had dug arrowroot with the women as soon as they could toddle. He thought Leki would be in his life forever. And then the stranger came, Bu, with his fine canoe and his promises of marriage gifts for Leki's family.

Girls usually married into other camps, but they didn't have to. Surely Leki didn't want to leave the camp and everyone she knew? He should have told her how he felt, even if he hadn't proved he could be a hunter yet.

Loa's hand tightened around his spear. He'd prove himself today! He felt like yelling at the sky. But you couldn't even speak on a pig hunt, in case the pigs heard you.

Slowly the rhythm of the hunt soothed him. This was his world. Every scent and shadow were as comfortable as his skin. The noises of the forest chittered around them — birds waking, cuscuses leaping from tree to tree. Only the hunters were silent, their skins dark as the dawn, their bare feet quiet on the leafy forest floor.

The world smelled of night-time and animals. He

wrinkled his nose at the scent of fruit bat — there must be a camp nearby — and the musky scent of giant rats. But there was another odour too ...

Loa stopped and held his hand up. The older hunters glanced at the ground, then back at Loa. Loa's grandfather made the hunting gesture that said: pig tracks?

Loa gestured to his nose. He'd smelled pig, not seen it. He stared at the leafy ground. Pig tracks must be here somewhere.

Over there! He bent down, examining them. One big pig, its prints pressed hard into the soil, and many little ones. A sow and its babies.

He exchanged glances with the others. A big sow protecting her piglets was more dangerous than a boar. Sows didn't have tusks, but their teeth were sharp. A big sow was stronger than a man. An angry sow might attack, not run. An angry sow could kill. The only safe way to catch a pig was to throw a net over it, then spear it as it fell tangled up in the net.

The sow's prints were fresh, and far apart. The sow was near and moving quickly, heading to the stream for a drink, perhaps ...

Loa lifted his head to sniff again, just as a giant sow charged out of a bush. A bunch of piglets squealed and ran towards their mother.

There was no time to net the sow now. She'd be on them in a heartbeat. Her teeth were curved and dark.

Deadly.

Loa stared as the tiny piggy eyes stared straight at him. She had chosen to attack him, the smallest of the hunters. He held his spear loosely. Even the strongest man couldn't throw a stone-tipped spear to pierce a pig's hide. You had to thrust with all your strength and weight behind the movement.

The sow came closer, closer ...

His grandfather yelled, trying to lure the pig away. Loa's father yelled too.

But this pig was Loa's.

Closer, closer. He could almost smell her breath, see each bristle on her hide. Vaguely he was aware of the other hunters yelling, nets held ready, of piglets squealing.

The sow lowered her head, her mouth open, ready to strike.

He lifted up his spear.

The sow struck it in full flight. Her rage drove the spear deeper and deeper into her neck. She screamed in fury and defiance.

Loa fought to steady his spear, using the sow's weight and speed against her. His muscles screamed as the sow lurched back and forth, trying to bite him.

She was too strong, even with his spear in her bleeding neck. Any moment now his spear would break ...

Suddenly the net landed on top of the furious sow. She stumbled. The hunters stabbed her with their spears, over and over. The sow struggled. She screamed a despairing warning to her piglets, defiant to the end.

At last the sow lay still.

Loa glanced around, panting. The piglets squealed helplessly in another net. His grandfather plunged his spear into their throats. The piglets gurgled, one by one, then lay still. His grandfather grinned. His hands and arms were streaked with blood, like Loa's.

Loa suddenly realised he was still alive. He had speared a pig! A charging sow! There was no place in the world he'd rather be than here.

He felt his grandfather's eyes on him, bright and proud. The old man reached down and untied the knife that hung among the leaves on the string around his waist.

'Here.' His grandfather pressed the knife into Loa's hand. He didn't say anything more. He didn't have to.

Loa gazed at the knife. It was the best knife in the camp. Grandfather had been given it as a bride price for his daughter, Loa's aunt, when she left their clan to marry a hunter from a clan up in the hills. The blade was obsidian, the sharpest stone in the world. An obsidian blade lasted forever.

For a moment he felt like dancing with the trees. But you didn't do that at a pig hunt either.

The sow was so massive it took four of them to lift her on a pole onto their shoulders. Loa went first, even though he was the youngest.

This prize was his.

Behind them the other hunters carried the piglets.

The sow was heavy, the sticky blood drawing flies. I'll have the teeth made into a necklace, he thought. When everyone ate pig meat this afternoon they'd know Loa the hunter had fed them.

The sun bobbed gold and heavy above the trees as they entered the camp, sending a spear of sunlight across the sea to their lagoon. Loa waited for the yells of admiration, the look on Leki's face.

But the camp was almost deserted. A couple of men too old to hunt tended the fire pit, its smoke drifting up into the sky. Small boys hauled up more driftwood. And the dogs, the slinking rubbish dogs, lifted their noses at the smell of pig.

The women and girls must be gathering tubers and fruit for the wedding feast. Leki wouldn't even see his sow till it was cooked inside the pit and handed round in sweet hot chunks. Maybe no one would even tell her who had speared it.

The joy of the hunt faded.

Loa helped his father and grandfather cut around the sow's anus, using his fine obsidian knife for the first time, then ripped open her belly. The three of them held the pig up by her front legs so the guts spilled out and didn't taint the meat. Over at the edge of the camp the rubbish dogs sniffed eagerly.

Let the dogs find their own feast, thought Loa. He looked around for something to throw at them. But the rocks were all in the cooking pit to heat up under the fire.

His muscles ached. His heart ached too. He followed the other hunters to the lagoon to wash off the pig's blood, then sat down in the shade against a tree, watching the men throw more wood into the fire pit.

At last Grandfather gave the sign to throw the sow onto the hot rocks. The fire would burn off her bristles and crisp her skin. Loa saw them drag the sow over the dirt, heard the thud as she landed on the rocks.

The men covered her in dirt with shell scoops to keep in the heat.

The piglets would go into the pit later; they didn't need as much cooking. Finally tubers would be added when the women came back, wrapped in arrowroot leaves to keep them moist and clean and to give them flavour. The last of the dirt would be piled on top of the pit oven and the whole thing left to cook till this afternoon. Bu and his friends' canoes would appear around the headland and the feast would begin ...

'Loa?'

Loa blinked. The little boy was his nephew, his older sister's oldest son.

'What do you want?' Couldn't the boy see he didn't want to talk?

'When can I hunt pigs?'

'When all your baby teeth are gone.'

'When will that be?'

Loa said nothing.

'Can I try your spear?'

'No!'

'But I want to hunt!'

'Little boys don't hunt.'

'We can hunt the rubbish dogs!' said the boy eagerly.

Loa almost laughed. You didn't 'hunt' rubbish dogs. You just killed them if you needed their meat to lure the sharks, or tied them up to take on long journeys in case you didn't find fish to eat instead.

Wild dogs could be dangerous. The clan always drew closer to the fire when the pack howled at night.

But a well-aimed stone was enough to keep a rubbish dog from coming too close.

The rubbish dogs nosed through the pig guts now.

It would serve the scavengers right if the boys caught them. Let Bu eat dog meat, instead of pig!

He tried to speak patiently to his nephew. 'You don't spear rubbish dogs. Just throw a net over them. Hunters need to learn how to net too,' he added.

The little boy almost bounced with happiness. 'We're going to catch the rubbish dogs!' he yelled to his friends.

Loa watched as the boy ran off to pull down a net from a sleeping platform.

He leaned back against the tree, shut his eyes and thought of Leki as the younger boys tiptoed towards the rubbish dogs, the net in their hands.

CHAPTER 3

# The Dog

The pig guts smelled warm, bloody and wonderful. The dog got her teeth into the meaty pig's heart before her brothers could. She pulled at it, determined to carry it off, to eat by herself under the trees.

Suddenly one of the older dogs growled a warning. She looked up as something fell from the sky.

The net covered her, almost blinding her. She tried to run but her paws caught in the holes. Her brothers struggled and clawed, trying to bite their way free.

'We caught the dogs!' yelled a boy. The other boys' feet thudded on the dirt as they danced around the net.

The dog tensed, waiting to bite if one came close enough.

CHAPTER 4

# Loa

'Loa?' It was his nephew again.

'What?'

'We netted the dogs! How do you tie them up?'

'Carefully,' said Loa. 'They'll bite your fingers off.'

'Loa! Show us how!'

Loa heaved himself to his feet. He was a man, a hunter. It was his duty to show the boys what to do. He trudged over to the heaving mass of dogs and net. 'You put your foot on their snout, see?' He stamped down on the biggest dog, a male. 'That way they can't bite. Now reach through the net and tie up the front paws. That's it. Now the hind paws. See how I tie up his jaws? There. You tie up the others.'

He stepped back, ready to help if it looked like the boys would be badly bitten. But despite yells and lunges they managed it. They stood back, staring as proudly at their three bound dogs as Loa had at his sow.

'Will Grandfather cook the dogs now?'

Not till it's time to put in the piglets, thought Loa. 'Go and ask him.'

He watched the boys run off again. Soon the women would be back. Bu and his friends would arrive with the gifts for Leki's family. Bu was a canoe maker, so a beautiful new canoe would be the main bride gift. But there'd be others: strings of beads and fish to add to the feast.

Everyone would sit and eat and eat, calling jokes, while Leki and Bu ...

Suddenly he couldn't stay here, with the smells of smoke and feasts.

He ran down to the beach. He jogged along the hard wet sand, away from the camp and the cooking pit, the boys and their laughter. Away from everything!

Small waves splashed at his ankles as the sea sucked in and out. He rounded the headland. The waves crashed high and long here, away from the protection of the reef and the lagoon.

At last he sank to his knees. The sand felt as hot as the sun above him. He didn't care. He put his face in his hands and thought of Leki.

He didn't know how long he'd sat on the beach when he heard Leki's voice.

'Loa?'

Loa scrambled to his feet. It was as though his dream had conjured her up.

But he had never seen Leki look like this. Her dark hair was hidden by a wig of dried grass, standing like rays of the sun. Her skirt was new bark cloth, faintly patterned with leaves. Ropes of shell beads hung from her neck and waist. She held a paperbark bag in one hand, bulging with shellfish gathered along the shore. She is already gathering food for Bu, he thought.

She was more beautiful than anyone he had ever seen.

He felt like a small boy, not the hunter who had killed a massive sow just that morning.

'Leki.' He walked up the hot sand towards her, trying to keep his voice steady. 'Don't leave your people to live with strangers! Your parents can't make you marry Bu. You could ... you could marry me.' His tongue felt tangled. 'I speared a sow today. Grandfather will tell your parents I'll be a great hunter too ...'

His voice died away as she smiled at him. It was the smile an older sister might give her brother. Suddenly she seemed years older than he was. 'Loa, I want to marry Bu.'

She said it so simply Loa knew that it was true.

It was as though a wave had leaped from the sea to slap his face. Bu was older, stronger. He had shown the uncles and grandfathers a new way to shape a canoe to give it better balance. His muscles had gleamed as he swung his adze.

How could a girl not love Bu?

That was the worst of all.

'I want to go back to Bu's clan too. Haven't you ever dreamed of new places, Loa? Something beyond the hunting ground and the lagoon?'

No, he thought. Why would I want to leave here?

Leki looked back down the beach towards the camp. The smoke from the cooking pit had vanished into faint shimmers in the air. She smiled, almost as though she no longer saw him. 'Go back to the feast.'

As though I'm a child to be told what to do, Loa thought bitterly.

'Bu might bring some of his sisters with him. Maybe you'll fancy one of them.'

'No!'

Her smile disappeared. 'Loa, don't be like this —'

'I'm going fishing!' he yelled. It was the first excuse he could think of.

She looked at him like she had when they were toddlers pretending their sticks were canoes in the lagoon. But at least she was seeing *him* now, not dreaming of Bu. 'You're stupid. No one will take out a canoe with you today. They'll want to be at the feast.'

He *was* being stupid. There was no need for fish, not with pig and dog in the fire pit. But he couldn't take his words back.

Leki wasn't the only one who could go to new places.

'I'll take the canoe out by myself. I'll paddle down the coast to the clan who lives beyond the giant-headland-near-the-sky. I'll come back with the most beautiful wife in the world. Two big, fat wives!'

'Loa.' She looked at him indulgently, as if he'd boasted he could climb up the pig-tusk path across the ocean to the moon.

He wondered if he had ever really known her. She was the most familiar thing in his life — and suddenly the strangest.

And even if he did bring back a wife, Leki would be gone with Bu.

She stood there on the beach, exotic in her golden-grass headdress. No matter how long he looked, he knew he would never find anyone as beautiful as her.

He tore his gaze away and ran back towards the camp.

CHAPTER 5

# The Dog

The dog's legs ached from the cords. She wanted to run, to whimper.

She couldn't do either. The cords held her jaws shut too.

The world smelled of death and pig blood. It would smell of dog blood soon too.

An old man limped over to the rubbish dogs. He grabbed her uncle by the cords that held his paws. The dog remembered her uncle bringing her monkey meat when she was a puppy; and sitting guarding the litter while the others hunted.

The old man slashed Uncle's throat. Suddenly Uncle was meat, not her uncle at all.

She wanted to howl, to whine. All she could do was shut her eyes or watch.

She watched. Perhaps, just perhaps, there was a chance to get away.

She wriggled her paws again. The cords still held them tight. She moved her jaws from side to side, but even that didn't lessen the bonds.

Only she and her brother were left now. She growled as the old man approached them. He grabbed her brother this time. The old man dragged him to the killing ground, then threw his body in the pit.

The old man made a noise. He sounded happy.

The dog stared at the lounging humans, at the heap of pig entrails, flies buzzing around them, at the waves lapping on the beach. She watched for any chance to struggle, to bite and run ...

She was next.

## CHAPTER 6

# Loa

The men dozed in the shade around the cooking pit; the boys were off somewhere. None of the women had come back.

No one noticed Loa grab his fishing spear. He jogged down to the lagoon where the canoes lay high on the sand, away from the reach of the tide. He tied his spear into the smallest craft. Canoes sank down almost to the level of the water when there was a pile of fish in them. You had to tie your spear on so it didn't float away.

The canoe needed two paddlers, but he could manage it alone. He was Loa, pig killer! He untied a bundle of dried pig bladders from one end of the canoe and filled them with fresh water from the stream, then fastened them carefully in the canoe too. His new knife hung on the cords around his waist.

What else did he need? Food?

He hadn't eaten all day; no one ate before a feast. But he'd be at the next clan's camp by nightfall. There'd be food there.

He hesitated. He'd never been to the giant-headland-near-the-sky, though his grandfather had found a wife there. You could only see the headland on clear days. What if it took more than an afternoon to paddle there or find the camp?

Of course he could find the clan! He only had to look for the smoke of their campfire. And if the journey took longer than he thought he could come ashore tonight to make a sleeping platform out of reach of crocodiles and rats. He could eat shellfish and long fat mangrove worms in the trees. The world was full of food.

Maybe he could spear a big fish as a present for the headland camp. A shark, perhaps ...

He bit his lip. He'd be alone on the water, with no one to look out for sharks. A shark could snap you right out of a canoe. A crocodile could too.

He needed a rubbish dog. Crocs and sharks liked rubbish dog more than man. Fishermen always took a rubbish dog on long voyages, so they could throw the dog out to any circling sharks.

A rubbish dog was the best food to take too. Even strips of salted shark went bad in the glare of the sea, but you could kill a tied-up dog to eat whenever you wanted to go ashore, or make a tiny cooking fire on board and roast it piece by piece.

He ran back to the camp. Some of the women had returned. They sat in the shade, laughing and talking, wrapping their tubers in arrowroot leaves. But there was no sign of Leki, or her mother, or his own mother either.

His mother would worry when he wasn't at the feast. That's what mothers did: they worried. But

Leki could explain where he'd gone. His mother would be glad when he brought back a wife, he told himself.

'Loa!' One of his friends gestured for him to come over and sit with them.

Loa pretended he didn't hear. He looked over to where the netted rubbish dogs had lain. Only one was left — a small female. She glared at him as he walked up to her.

'You'll do.' He picked her up by the cords that bound her paws and carried her upside down.

The dog struggled, but she didn't make any sound. Rubbish dogs didn't make much noise: just growls, if you came near their pups, or long slow howls at night. This one didn't even whimper. Her jaws were tied too tightly.

He slung the dog into his canoe, then lashed her securely to the side next to his spear so no wave could wash her away.

He hesitated.

This was a big thing — to leave his clan, to try to find a wife all by himself. Young men went off to find wives, even sometimes stealing them. But not alone.

Should he wait? Ask some of his friends to come with him tomorrow?

Deep down he realised he didn't want to go at all. He didn't want a wife from a different clan. He wanted to be at the feast as everyone ate his pig meat and exclaimed; he wanted to make his pig's-teeth necklace; he wanted to hunt pig again in a few days' time.

But he had told Leki he would go. He wasn't going to hang around the edges of her feast, like a rubbish dog looking for her scraps of attention.

He had to go! Now!

He pushed the canoe over the sand, through the first waves, then clambered in. He began to paddle across the lagoon, towards the reef and the sea beyond.

Someone shouted from the shore. He looked back, but he was already too far away to see who it was. He waved, then turned back to paddling.

The rubbish dog stared at him from the end of the canoe.

CHAPTER 7

# The Dog

Her back was bruised where the bony boy had flung her into the canoe. Her legs ached from being tied in one position. She needed to drink, to howl. But she was tied too tight to move.

She sniffed the salt water, trying to find familiar smells. It wasn't right to be out here on the sea. It wasn't right to be tied up either, or to be alone away from the other dogs, with just a boy. Bony Boy, she thought, not a pup but not grown up either.

She wriggled to ease the pain in her legs. Suddenly her muzzle felt a sharp edge on the canoe. Cautiously she rubbed her nose along it.

The rope moved, just a little.

If she could get the cords off her muzzle then she could bite through the cords that held her paws. She could bite Bony Boy too.

She could be free.

But first she needed to move the cords. She rubbed again, slowly, keeping her eyes on Bony Boy as he paddled.

# CHAPTER 8

# Loa

The breeze ruffled the surface of the lagoon. Loa paddled towards the white water that led out to the open ocean. The sea was rougher beyond the reef, but he needed to leave the safety of his own lagoon if he was going to paddle along the coast to the headland clan.

He tried to think of returning with a bride of his own. She'd have plump legs and a little round tummy, to show how good she was at finding tubers and catching birds ...

Reality spat in his face with the windblown spray from the waves on the reef. How could he get a wife like that, when even Leki — who had known him all her life and his family's worth — had chosen someone else?

In a few years, when he'd proved his worth as a hunter, he could have his choice of wives. He'd be taller and stronger, instead of being only just a man. But now?

He gritted his teeth. He was already a hunter! Hadn't he caught the sow this morning and with his first spear thrust too?

He'd show the men of the giant-headland-near-the-sky clan just how strong he was, despite his age. He'd hunt pig with them. Show them Loa the hunter! They'd see his fine fish spear, his obsidian knife ...

The canoe bucked as it reached the rougher water beyond the lagoon. He paddled out far enough from the reef to be safe from the waves that might suck him onto the jagged teeth of the coral or swamp him in their froth and tumble, then turned the canoe expertly and began to paddle parallel to the reef and the beach. The sun beat hot on his back. It was almost midday now. Back at the camp the women would have baskets of wild figs. The young men would be dozing in the shade till the feast was cooked.

The coastline began to curve. Soon he wouldn't be able to see their campsite, the dark figures on the beach, the faint hint of smoke in the air. He looked ahead.

He couldn't bear to look back now.

CHAPTER 9

# The Dog

The day grew hotter. The light bounced from the sea, brighter than the sky. She wanted to pant, but the cords that held her were too tight.

Where were her brothers and sisters, the older dogs? Where were the smells of soil and bones and trees?

She had never been so hot before. Never so thirsty. There wasn't even the scent of fresh water out here. She didn't like these smells, or the way the world bounced beneath her.

Her thirst grew worse. She could feel her strength ebbing like the waves from the sand, but she forced herself to keep rubbing the cords around her jaws against the wood of the canoe.

She had to get free.

She didn't try to think how she would get back to land after she had freed her paws. Her world had narrowed to one fierce thought.

Attack the boy.

CHAPTER 10

# Loa

It was mid-afternoon when he felt the current change, tugging at the canoe. It was as though the reef was pulling him towards it.

He was far beyond anywhere he'd paddled before. The uncles hadn't said what winds and currents they'd faced when they'd paddled to the camp on the giant-headland-near-the-sky. It was best to show a boy how to do a new thing, not tell him.

He should have waited till tomorrow, tried to persuade one of the older, more experienced men to come with him. Two canoes and four men, perhaps, or even three canoes. Three canoes were safest. Yet here he was, one boy and one canoe out on the broad expanse of the sea, alone ...

Except for a rubbish dog. He glanced back at it.

The rubbish dog lay on her side. She had been scratching against the edge of the canoe, but she stopped moving as soon as he looked around.

She must be thirsty, he thought. He'd forgotten she'd need water, here in the glare of the sun. A dead dog wasn't as useful as a live one. Sharks liked their prey fresh. But there was no time now to give her water. He needed to keep the canoe from the reef, or they'd both be dead.

He turned the canoe out towards the open sea, not directly opposing the rip but at an angle to it, and began to paddle as strongly as he could.

His arms ached as he fought the current. At last the drag on the canoe lessened. He relaxed, undid one of the water bladders, then took a deep drink.

The water cleared his head. He crawled over to the rubbish dog, then dripped a little water into his hand and held it out to her.

The cords around her muzzle wouldn't let her open her mouth wide enough to bite him, but were now loose enough for her to put out her tongue a little. She lapped, feebly at first, and then more eagerly.

He filled his hand again, then tied the bladder up, instinctively cautious. He knew she wanted more. He wanted more water too. But they were far from land. So far away that the trees looked as small as leaf ants.

It scared him a little. He had never been so far out to sea before. Canoes were made for fishing in the lagoon, or short voyages around a cape, not for facing the vast sea. He'd imagined creeping around the beaches till he found the headland camp, not drifting alone in the vast blue like this.

He forced the fear away and scanned the waves between him and the shore, trying to see if there was a calm area that looked like a break in the reef.

There had to be one soon!

But he hadn't even been paddling for half a day yet. Maybe there'd be a break soon ...

Or maybe there wouldn't. Maybe you had to paddle a whole day in this direction, just to find a place where you could safely take a canoe in to shore. And he'd set out when the daylight was already half over. He'd be out here in the roughness and vastness of the open sea at night, alone.

He twirled the paddle slowly from one side to the other, so the canoe stayed pretty much in one place while he considered. If he turned back now he'd be back at his own camp with enough light to find it, especially with the big fire for songs and storytelling after the feast. You could see a glow like that from a long way away.

Or he could keep going and hope that he'd find a place to go ashore soon, even if he hadn't reached the giant-headland-near-the-sky.

But reefs could be tricky, with outcrops here or there, waves and rips and sandbanks. He'd have to work out the best way through, keeping a sharp eye out for the unexpected, whether that was a rogue wave or a cruising shark.

And he was tired. Up in the first grey light for the pig hunt; carrying the sow back to camp; paddling for so long.

He scanned the coast again, looking ahead and then looking behind him, trying to make up his mind whether to keep going, or head back.

And then he stared. Billows of grey pushed up from the eastern horizon.

Storm! The worst storms came from the east: the wild winds that tore up forests, when all you could do was huddle together in a cave till the fury of the storm was gone. But it wasn't the Thunder Season yet, though that was coming next. It wasn't even the Rain Season, with its sudden downpours, when the sky turned to solid water and then, just as suddenly, sunlight returned.

Sometimes the seasons came early, but the aunties had a pretty good idea when that would happen. The trees told them by the way they flowered or fruited. The aunties hadn't said anything about an early Wet this year.

So this was just a storm. A little storm.

Probably.

But any storm would be bad out here in the rough water, in a shallow canoe. He had to get to safety. Fast.

He had no choice now. He had to turn back and get near the camp, into the seas he was familiar with, before the storm hit.

He manoeuvred the canoe around. He had only tried to paddle half a dozen strokes before he realised.

The current was pushing him away from the camp. He hadn't noticed because he'd been trying to go the same way. It was going to take him twice the time, twice the energy, to get back home.

The grey clouds filled all the low horizon now. This is going to be a bad one, he thought, just as the first gust of wind hit. It was so hard it almost blew the canoe over on its side.

This morning he'd thought the sea was his to play with. Loa the pig killer was lord of the sea too.

Now the sea and sky were vast, and he was small.

A current tugging west. A wind blowing him west too. He couldn't paddle against them both.

Behind him the rubbish dog whimpered as though she sensed the danger. He gritted his teeth as he turned the canoe back yet again.

Once again, he had no choice. He had to keep paddling west, into the unknown, hoping that soon he'd see a place to go ashore.

Soon, he prayed. Let me find safety soon.

CHAPTER 11

# The Dog

The air was wind and water. Waves tossed the canoe this way and that, the cords that bound her to the canoe digging into her each time. Her fur was wet. A puddle grew at the bottom of the canoe over her paws, her tummy. She had to close her eyes to stop the salt sting of spray.

Every instinct yelled, 'Danger! Hide!'

There was nowhere to hide in the canoe.

The dog kept on scraping at the cords. Scraping. Scraping.

CHAPTER 12

# Loa

The sky was grey. The air was grey too. Rain lashed about them, thrown by the wind. Waves reared over the canoe, splashing down so he had to use his cupped hands to bail frantically to stop the canoe from sinking, then dig the paddle into the sea to manoeuvre them around the next wave, and the next.

The waves weren't Wild Wind high. They weren't even Big Storm high. But they were higher than a shallow canoe; higher than a frightened boy could cope with.

But there was no choice. And I am not a boy, he reminded himself. This morning I was a hunter. I fought the sow! I can fight the storm now.

The afternoon was swallowed by the night.

Time vanished. The world vanished too. There were only the waves, the wind, the rain. He had no idea how he kept the canoe afloat. He only knew that he had.

So far.

CHAPTER 13

# The Dog

A cord snapped next to her muzzle. She rubbed at the other cords, keeping a cautious eye on Bony Boy. But he was frantically paddling, his back to her.

The other cords slid free.

She stretched her jaws, feeling the pain and stiffness, then bent her head. Her teeth worked at the cords that held her paws.

The wind screamed like a dying pig around them. The canoe bucked, the spray lashed from side to side. Bony Boy urgently scooped the water from around them and threw it back into the storm.

She could do nothing about the wind or water. Instead she bit the cords. It was hard to get a grip — the rocking, swaying boat kept rolling her back and forth and the storm blinded her. Each time the canoe lurched and rolled she was sure she would be swept from the fragile little shell, tumbling helplessly with bound legs into the water.

The cords around her paws snapped.

She tried to move her legs. Nothing happened. For a moment she felt panic. She tried again.

This time they moved, stiff and so painful she

whimpered, then glanced at Bony Boy to see if he had heard.

He hadn't. His back was to her as he heaved and bucketed against the storm.

She tried to stand. At last she realised it wasn't just the weakness of her legs preventing her from standing. There were more cords about her back, holding her to the canoe. She knew to leave them as they were: her only security now was the bucking canoe and Bony Boy, desperately bailing and paddling. Waves reared about them, capped with foam.

Just for now, she let the cords stay.

CHAPTER 14

# Loa

The air was dark with more than storm now: black sky; black water all around. Even the waves' foam was dark. His world had shrunk to each battering of water, tilting his body frantically each time the canoe was shoved onto its side, brief gulps of air in between the world of water.

It took minutes, perhaps, to realise that although the wind still snarled and the foam still whipped across his skin, the canoe was hardly moving. It had lodged somehow, leaning to the right.

His body knew it before his mind had grasped it. Land! They had come aground, somehow, somewhere ...

He reached out a hand into the darkness and felt water rip and tear, still too deep for his fingers to find sand.

He stood uncertainly, then lowered one leg over the side of the canoe. Sand sucked and wriggled under his foot, stirred by the force of waves.

Which way was land, and which was the open sea? He risked pulling the canoe back towards the ocean. But every moment he stayed here he risked being slammed by another larger wave. The storm had dumped him here. It could tear him away too.

He reached his other leg down, holding onto the edge of the canoe. He took one step, then almost unconsciously pulled against the ocean's tug. If the sea wanted him *that* way, he would go *this* ...

He dragged the canoe with him. The water swirled around his thighs, his knees and finally his ankles.

He had no strength, no sight, no breath. It didn't matter. He kept on going anyway.

Another step. Another and another, digging his feet into wet sand. At last the only water came from the sky, not the sea. He could hear the crash of waves and the growl and swirl of the currents behind him. But wherever he was, he was beyond it now.

He sank down onto the wet sand, then roused himself, and forced himself to scrabble into the canoe again. Vaguely he thought that it was probably high tide now, but he could easily have lost track of time. The tide might still rise higher, or the storm might bring even larger waves. It was wet and cramped in the canoe, but if the waves were to find him again he was safer here.

His foot touched something. Something wet and furry, that shivered.

The rubbish dog.

The rubbish dog was still in the canoe. He reached blindly into the darkness. The water bladders were still there too, held fast by their cords, just like the rubbish dog and his spear.

He still had food then, a rubbish dog. Fresh water. He had weapons too.

He let his eyes close, though the darkness behind his lids was no greater than the night and storm. Suddenly he slept, as though a war axe had bashed him on his head.

CHAPTER 15

# The Dog

*A large sandbank in the great ocean, the Dry Season*

The rain stopped. The clouds fled past, leaving the star-swept sky clear. The dog watched Bony Boy sleep in the darkness. He lay on his back, his mouth open, his eyes shut.

She stretched cautiously, ready to run or snap if he moved. He gave a half snore, half cry, then breathed quietly again.

The dog lifted her nose and took in the smells around them. Land and sea, but much more sea than land. This land was a drift of sand in the ocean, no more. No smell of trees. Worse: no scent of fresh water.

Only one cord bound her to the canoe now. It didn't take long to bite through it.

She leaped from the canoe, feeling it shift slightly as she did. Still Bony Boy didn't move. She trod carefully through the star-dappled darkness up to the highest point of this tiny piece of solid ground. She lay down, keeping her nose pointed towards Bony Boy and the canoe, so that she'd know if either of them moved. She shut her eyes and allowed herself to snooze, her ears pricked, ready for what the dawn would bring.

Bony Boy slept as the far horizon grew grey instead of black. The dog gazed around. The waves had crept back across the sand, now the storm was gone.

She padded down to the water's edge, her ears still pricked in case Bony Boy moved, or a crocodile lurched from the water. It didn't take long to trot around the island.

It was pretty much as she had smelled it during the night: a long drift of sand above the waves. But there was a new meat smell now. She nosed around the seaweed and tangles of branches and leaves, then pounced.

A dead seagull!

She was more thirsty than hungry, but she needed to eat too. She carried the dead bird up to the top of the island again, then lay down with it between her paws. She nosed off the feathers, then bit into the flesh, enjoying crunching the bones. The salt-sodden feathers stung her lips and tongue.

She lifted her nose again, hoping that, somehow, there'd be the scent of fresh water. But there was just the sea and Bony Boy and the canoe.

She had never been so alone. There had always been the pack: the big female with her pups, the top dog, the uncles and aunts, the pups, toddling and learning to hunt. Even when she couldn't see them she knew where they were by their smell; knew where they'd been, what they were doing. She could smell where dogs had been for generations leaving their scent by trees and rocks. Her world was full of dog, if you knew how to smell it.

This world was empty.

How could you be a dog without a pack?

The pack would find her, she decided. There had to be dogs, even here. There had always been dogs.

She put her head on her paws and waited.

CHAPTER 16

# Loa

He woke with a start, looking up at the blue sky. Where was he? His tongue was too fat for his mouth, his lips swollen and cracked from the salt water.

He stared around him. No green tree shadows, no birdsong, no rustle of leaves. No mutters from the other members of the clan, no babies crying.

He sat up, feeling the roughness of the canoe around him, and remembered.

The storm. The waves, the frantic tugging of the canoe up onto the beach ...

He looked around. It wasn't a beach, not really. Beaches gave way to trees. Beaches had streams of fresh water.

This was just a low hill of sand, bright white in the blue of sea. In another storm it might vanish, or perhaps get bigger.

No trees. No streams. Just ... He stared.

Just the rubbish dog, sitting on top of the hill, her fur almost the colour of the sand, her eyes staring down at him.

He swallowed. There was a story passed down among the mothers of how a rubbish dog had taken a baby once. But that had been so long ago no one was sure if it was true.

The rubbish dogs knew that if they attacked a human, the other humans would attack back. But there was no one to help him now.

This rubbish dog could leap down and tear his throat open.

The rubbish dog was almost gold in the sun. She didn't move.

Loa looked back at the canoe. The water bladders were still there, and his spear. He automatically tipped the canoe over to empty the sea water from the bottom, untied the spear and held it at the ready, one eye on the motionless dog. He used his other hand to untie one of the bladders, then felt the cool trickle of fresh water against his lips.

It was the most wonderful thing he had ever tasted.

Above him the dog lifted her head. She gazed at him: she could smell the water.

Loa retied the neck of the water bladder. He glanced around again, searching the horizon.

Land! He felt his heart beat as he gazed at the green smudge. The storm had pushed the canoe for so long last night he had been afraid that he'd be so far from land he wouldn't even be able to see it. But there it was, a day's paddle away, over to the ...

He caught his breath. To the south. He felt the heat of the morning sun on his left side. It *was* the morning sun too: he knew he hadn't slept all day and, anyway, the evening sun was redder than the sun of morning.

Land to the north, east or even west could be home, but no one had ever seen land to the south. Yet there it was.

He shut his eyes. When he opened them the green smudge was still there. Land.

He tried to think. His head was dizzy from hunger and weariness, despite the sleep and the drink of water. Hadn't someone told a story about land to the south?

Old Uncle, that was it — a story about how Uncle's grandfather had seen smoke in the southern sky. The smoke had billowed up for days, as though there was a huge fire.

And, no, said Uncle sternly, it wasn't a cloud. His grandfather was not a fool. If there was smoke from the south there must be land too ...

Loa gazed at the green smudge. Green meant trees. Were there also cliffs, mountains, a lagoon? But already the sun was glinting on the water and it was impossible to make out any details through the glare.

He sat back in the canoe. There was still a hand's depth of water in it, seeped out of the wet wood, but he wanted its familiarity again, even if it was drier on the sand.

Land to the south, a day's paddle away. He had water. He even had food, if he speared the dog, or maybe he could spear a fish in the shallows here.

Or he could paddle north, and hope he found land there.

But what if he didn't? Loa had never paddled more than a few beaches from home, but others had. The uncles told stories of how the land stopped after so many days paddling to the east, or so many days paddling to the west.

What if the storm had blown him so far west that if he paddled north he would miss his land? Or maybe the land was there, but the storm had flung him too far to paddle home? He looked at his water bladders. They'd last him two days, maybe. How many days could you go without water, with the heat and glare of the sun reflected from the sea?

How many days and nights could he paddle without sleep? If he slept the tides might wash him back the way he'd come. After all, they'd already brought him here.

He looked down at his canoe. It was water sodden. Canoes rode low in the water at the best of times. Now it would be only a few handspans above the smallest waves. A shark could leap up and grab him. Sharks were always hungry after storms. Or a crocodile might grab him when he came near to land.

He looked at the rubbish dog again, wishing she was still safely tied in the end of the canoe, shark bait, crocodile bait, to keep him safe.

How had she got free? Chewing the cords, he supposed. A clever dog. But not clever enough to get away from his spear. Not on a tiny island, with nowhere to run.

He needed to drink again. But fresh water meant life or death now.

He looked back at the thin green line southwards, then at the blank blue of sky and sea that made up the rest of the horizon. Every moment he waited here meant it was longer before he had a chance of reaching land, and water.

Which way? North, to the wide blue nothing? South, towards the green? Take a chance that land might grow from the seamless blue of sea and sky, or paddle towards where he knew land was?

It isn't, he thought, really a choice at all.

He stood. His legs trembled as he jumped clumsily from the canoe. He looked at the dog and pushed up his spear. He could eat raw meat if he had to. Maybe the rubbish dog's blood would ease his thirst as well. His hand trembled as he tried to aim the spear. If he missed she might attack him. He'd be defenceless, his spear too far away to grab. He took another drink of water, and felt steadier.

Now he could kill the dog.

CHAPTER 17

# The Dog

The dog rested her head on her paws on her sand dune and watched Bony Boy drink. He was the only familiar thing in this new world.

There were no dogs here. No dogs would be able to come across the sea either. If she wanted to find her pack again she was going to have to get into the canoe and let Bony Boy take her back. The canoe meant pain and heat and thirst. It meant being with a human. But being alone was worse.

She did the only thing she could think of.

She rolled over on her back, her legs in the air, her paws limp. It was the 'roll over' that meant the other dog was boss, that you'd do what you were told, let them have the best of the food, the first drink of water. She was trying to say to Bony Boy, 'Let me back in the canoe. I'll do whatever you want.'

She didn't think he'd understand. Humans didn't understand dog things.

But what else could she do?

CHAPTER 18

# Loa

Loa stared at the rubbish dog. He'd never seen a dog roll over on its back like that. Rubbish dogs were yellow shadows at the edge of camp, sneaking, chewing, jumping.

The rubbish dog gave a sharp whine. That was strange too. She rolled back over onto her tummy — slowly, so he knew she wasn't about to leap. She put her head down on her paws and began to creep on her belly along the sand towards him.

It was the weirdest thing he had ever seen.

Was the dog trying to get closer so she could attack him? Suddenly he saw small white feathers in her fur and a pile of larger white feathers up on the sand. She had eaten a seagull.

He felt a flash of jealousy. The dog had eaten and he hadn't.

He lifted the spear again.

The dog kept crawling towards him.

He took a few paces back, to see what she would do, then watched amazed as she jumped into the canoe. She lay with her head on her paws again for a few moments, then began to sniff a water bladder.

'No!' He raised his spear. But the dog backed off at the anger in his voice.

Boy and dog looked at each other.

Slowly, very slowly, he reached down and untied one of the water bladders. He emptied a little into his hand, and reached out to her.

He wasn't sure why he did it. The rubbish dog would bite his hand. She would grab the water bladder and drag it back up the sand dune. She would ...

The rubbish dog crept forwards, still on her belly. He felt her tongue lick the water from his hand.

It tickled.

Suddenly he wished someone could see him, alone on a sandbank in the middle of the sea, with an untied rubbish dog licking water from his hand. Of course, if there was anyone to see, he wouldn't *be* alone.

The rubbish dog looked up at him, her brown eyes pleading. She wanted more water.

He couldn't kill the dog now. He wasn't sure why. He was pretty sure he might kill her, some other time. But not right now. And if he gave her more water she would be more likely to leave the bladders alone. Besides, the other one was still full. That far shore must be less than a day's paddle away, with the wind behind him, pushing him towards the land.

He trickled more water into his hand. Again the dog drank, and again and again. At last she put her head on her paws, as though to say she'd had enough.

He drank the rest, squeezing out the last drops, then tied the limp empty bladder to the canoe. He might need it again if he could find fresh water to fill it. He assessed the wind, the tide — heading out, just past the turn, he reckoned — then took a last regretful look at the sandbank. It had saved their lives, but it would kill them if they stayed there.

They needed to go now.

He bent down and pushed the canoe out into the waves. He half expected the rubbish dog to jump out as soon as he moved the canoe. But instead she stood and walked back a couple of steps, turning around and around, then sat on her haunches, facing him, exactly where she needed to be to balance his weight when he leaped into the canoe.

A good omen? Or was he crazy, heading out to an unknown land over unknown seas, with a rubbish dog?

No. He had been crazy yesterday — or at least foolish anyhow. He wondered if anyone had missed him yet, if Leki ...

He tried to pull a sheet of bark over the image of Leki and Bu, of home and family, the leftovers of the feast. He jumped into the canoe, steadied it, then began to paddle towards the thin line of green.

CHAPTER 19

# The Dog

It felt strange, being free in a canoe. She quickly learned to move to help steady it every time a wave slapped them. She'd have liked to doze, but the bottom of the canoe kept filling up with water, so she couldn't put her head down. Bony Boy kept scooping the water out, in between sessions of paddling.

The sun rose higher. It grew hot, but not as hot as when she'd been tied up the day before. The spray dampened her fur; and now she could move the wind cooled her. Every so often Bony Boy stopped and offered her water — just a handful, but it was enough — then drank himself.

The smell of land grew closer.

It took her a while to realise what was wrong. The land smelled ... different. Not just of new things, but the absence of things that should be there too.

No pig smell. No dogs.

But it was land. For now, that was enough.

## CHAPTER 20

# Loa

Today everything went right. It was as though the dog was a good luck sign. Crawling to him, sitting there at the other end of the canoe. If only the dog could help him paddle!

He grinned. He had enough strangeness to cope with: he didn't want a paddle suddenly appearing in the dog's mouth, to add to the general weirdness of it all.

The wind pushed exactly where he wanted to go. The currents carried them too. He was making at least twice the speed he had yesterday, maybe more.

I am a sea eagle, he thought. I am a gull, spearing across the sea.

Something scraped at the side of the canoe. A branch. He pulled it up, and stared. The leaves were unfamiliar: curved like the water moon, a dull sea-washed green. He let the branch slide back into the water.

But the branch was also a good sign. The tide which had brought the branch out here would help him back where it had come from.

He kept on paddling.

* * *

The sun climbed higher. At every extra handspan of the sky he stopped to drink and give the rubbish dog water too. The wind dropped about noon, but he was close enough to see the shape of the land now — cliffs and, far off, the silver shimmer of a beach.

No rough seas or coral reefs. He would have grinned if he hadn't been so tired and thirsty. He changed course slightly, away from the cliffs, aiming for the beach. He had paddled for another part span when he realised he wasn't going to get there.

A current had caught him again.

This one was as strong as yesterday's. It swept him away from the bright beach with its comfortable rolling waves, back towards the cliffs.

But it wasn't just a solid line of rock, he saw with relief as the canoe drew closer. What had looked like one giant cliff face further out at sea was really a series of bluffs, separated by coves of mangroves — long stretches of grey mud dappled with small trees.

It would be better to land on a beach, with firm sand, than in the smelly sucking squelch of mangroves. It would be harder to see a crocodile in mangroves too — and harder to get away. But on the other hand the waves inside the mangrove coves were only ripples. It would be a smooth landing, with no risk of being dumped, canoe and all, by the waves. And where there were mangroves there was usually a stream. Fresh water ...

He let the current take him now, paddling only enough to keep the canoe steady. He put his hand to his eyes to cut out the glare of the sea. No sign of people; no smoke from campfires. He hadn't seen any smoke all day.

Maybe this was an island, with no people on it? If so, it must be a massive one. Or it might be the land of ghosts? He shivered, then told himself not to be stupid. A land of ghosts wouldn't have seagull droppings splattered down the cliffs. They'd be ghost gulls. Ghost gulls wouldn't leave white droppings.

He glanced at the rubbish dog. Her eyes were half shut, but her ears were cocked, alert. The aunties said that the rubbish dogs howled when they heard the ghosts of the ancestors.

The dog wasn't howling now. And any crocodile would grab the rubbish dog, not him.

He hoped.

Nearer, and nearer still ... He could no longer see the beach, just the cliffs, bulging brown and streaked white with droppings, and the long stretch of mangroves. The current still pulled him, but he was still able to steer the canoe enough to avoid the cliffs.

This was going to be easy.

CHAPTER 21

# The Dog

She let her nose speak to her. She could smell mud, trees, fresh water, turtle. She could smell crocodile too, but not close enough to be a danger. A breeze blew from the land, bringing more scents from further away. Rock, strange animals ...

Nearer and nearer.

The canoe lurched. Bony Boy yelled in surprise. The canoe twisted like the water was a giant hand twirling a stick. The sea surged towards her.

# CHAPTER 22

# Loa

*The north coast of the great south land, the Dry season*

He saw the jagged rock just before the canoe struck — dark rock like rotting teeth just below the surface of the water, hidden in the ripples from the breeze.

He pushed frantically with the paddle to edge the canoe away. It was too late. The canoe's prow hit the rock. Suddenly he breathed water, not air. He forced the water from his nose and mouth, along with precious bubbles of air, as the world exploded into pain.

Had he hit the rock? No. The canoe had struck his leg. It still bobbed above him. He pushed with his arms and suddenly the canoe was gone, and he was over the rocks into the smoother water by the shore.

But his leg ... even that small movement had made him almost black out with pain. He gagged, spitting out salt water. How could he swim without moving his leg? But he had to.

He stroked his arm through the water. The movement kept his head above water, at least. Every sway made him hot and cold at the same time. He refused to let the pain take him. It was agony: impossible to keep going. But he did. Slowly, slowly, the land came towards him.

At last he saw mud below him, and the small stalks of submerged mangroves, and then trees growing in the water. He grabbed a branch, trying to haul himself upright on his one good leg. The mud sucked at his foot. The water was still up to his knees. The tree bent, but it held.

He was still several spear lengths from the muddy shore. He tried to hop, hauling himself from tree to tree, keeping to the firm areas of balled tree root so he didn't sink into the mud. At last the sea was behind him.

He let himself look down at his leg. Blood oozed from a cut on his thigh. His knee was crooked, puffed up like a water-filled bladder. Knees don't look like that, he thought vaguely.

The mud and trees stretched around him. Low tide. Crocodile tide. He had to get out of the mangroves before the rising sea sucked him back into the swirl of water. Had to get to high ground, away from crocodiles.

Then all at once the world was cold. Then nothing.

CHAPTER 23

# The Dog

Water surged and bubbled about her. The dog fought and found herself rising. Her head broke into sunlight and she gulped air. She'd never swum before, but instinctively her legs began to move the right way, through the water, over to the shore.

She struggled to keep her head above water, panting, spluttering as the waves splashed her nose. At last she felt mud under her paws. She fought her way through the last of the water, the mud sucking at her. She finally found firm ground on a ball of mangrove root. She shook herself dry, then looked for Bony Boy and the canoe.

The canoe was floating down the coast, out past the place where it had overturned. Bony Boy lay in the mud. He didn't move, but she thought he was alive.

She was glad. In this world of strange smells he at least was familiar. But she needed water. Her paws trembled with weakness. Her throat and mouth hurt.

Water!

She lifted her nose. Yes, there was its scent again. She bounded out across the mangroves, pushing her body with the last of her strength, too fast for her paws to sink into the mud; too fast also, she hoped, for the crocodile she could smell somewhere not too far away to grab her.

The mud ended in a broken cliff, steps and stairs of crumbling rock. It was steep, but not too steep for a sure-footed dog to find a way. She began to climb, letting her nose lead her to the water.

# CHAPTER 24

# Loa

He awoke to mud — and water nibbling at his toes. The tide had risen.

He looked down at his leg. Blood dribbled down his skin. His knee was a swollen thundercloud, blue and purple, the size of a piglet's head. His foot poked out at a strange angle.

The world swam as though he was still underwater. Too much sun, he thought vaguely. Pain. No food. Not enough water.

He looked around for his canoe ... and then remembered. The edge of this land had grabbed him, had pulled him from the canoe.

He gazed desperately around the small cove. The canoe had vanished. Perhaps it had washed up on one of the beaches or other coves. Perhaps it was already bobbing out at sea, or even sunk. It didn't matter. He couldn't search for it, not when every movement made him dizzy.

The canoe was gone. So were his water bladders and his spear.

What did he have?

He looked down at himself. A boy's body, not a

man's, trembling with weakness. The cords around his waist, his knife. No family. No friends. A strange land, and empty hands.

Even the rubbish dog had left him.

It was too much to take in.

One thing was left. Survive. Get away from the mangroves, where crocodiles lurked unseen in the mud. Find fresh water.

If he could make it up to the cliffs behind the cove he should find both water and safety. Crocs didn't like to climb. This mangrove must be fed by a stream or a swamp. Either would mean fresh water.

He pulled himself upright. The black tide of pain swept over him. He ignored it, holding onto the stunted mangrove tree. He took one step and then another, almost falling as he grabbed the next tree.

This wasn't working. He couldn't keep going if every time he moved he collapsed with pain. He gritted his teeth, broke off two thick branches, then untied the ropes at his waist. He used the cords to tie the branches to his leg, above and below the knee. At least that should keep his knee from twisting every time he tried to hop.

He hesitated, then tied the knife back on the cord above his knee too. It would be easy to lose the knife in the mud if he carried it in his hand.

The knife was his only link with home. Without it he was an animal, outcast, with no pack to help him.

He tried putting some weight on his bad leg. The pain was as bad, but the feeling that the world was going to fade away about him was less. He could hop like this. A little way, at least.

He began again. Hop, dragging his other leg, hop, grab. Hop, hop, grab.

Suddenly he saw it: a brown log, the colour of the mud, lying in the shadows of the trees.

But this log was crocodile.

Crocs were lazy. They waited for you and lunged. Grandfather said a good hunter didn't hunt, but waited. Crocs were the best hunters of all.

He edged further away, slowly, keeping his eyes on the croc. If it wanted to the giant croc could catch him easily, destroy him in one powerful snap of its jaws. But maybe it had fed recently.

Had it eaten the rubbish dog?

His knee throbbed. His head throbbed too, his fear easing as step by step he managed to get further from the waiting croc.

The cliffs grew nearer: grey-brown with lighter stripes, crumbling at the base. He made for the most inland point before the cliffs began. There was still no sign of a stream or river, but he could dig out a hole in a freshwater swamp, and let it fill. That would be enough.

At least these mangroves were like the ones at home, even if the cliffs were strange. He could see gulls' footprints in the mud, the tiny holes that meant mud crabs below, and mud worms. There was food here.

And the swish mark of a tail. Another crocodile! It had been this way. Not long ago either — water still hadn't seeped into the swish mark. Was it watching him, waiting to grab him, to tear his flesh? High above, a buzzard soared black against the sky. Loa was food for others too. But he had no spear now to protect him, no friends, no grandfather to help him hunt. He felt even more alone than in the storm. He forced himself forwards.

Nearer and nearer ...

Then he saw the water. A thin seep from the cliffs, just enough to wet the rock. Not enough water to gather in his hands. No other water, except the sea behind. When the Wet Season came there'd be a river here. But not at this time of year. He limped towards it. He could almost feel it on his salt-cracked lips. He bent to touch the wet rock. But his knee wouldn't let him crouch. He sat awkwardly in the mud.

He licked the rock. His tongue could taste the water, taste the lichen on the rock. But it wasn't even enough to wet his mouth.

If he didn't drink soon he'd die. If he stayed here, weaker and weaker, a crocodile would get him, tonight, tomorrow, as soon as it was hungry.

Cliffs above him, too steep to climb with a leg that wouldn't work. Mangroves around him. And beyond them, the sea.

He wanted to cry. But a hunter didn't cry. Perhaps his body had no water for tears either. His head buzzed, like it was full of bees.

He looked around, vaguely hoping that somehow a canoe of fishermen might appear on the waves; that he'd see smoke rising behind the cliffs and people near enough to hear his yells.

But there was nothing. Nothing but rock and mud and sea and sky.

The buzzard flew lower, peering down at him.

He stood up again, holding onto the cliff to steady himself. He clambered a few spear lengths up onto a jagged ledge of rock, pulling with his arms, letting his useless leg dangle behind. The ledge was just wide enough for him to lie down.

The ledge wasn't high enough to keep him safe from a crocodile, not if it really wanted him. But at least he wasn't lying in the mud, as though to say, 'Come and eat me!' He shut his eyes.

Maybe after a rest he'd be able to think what to do. Maybe it would rain. He could open his mouth and let it fill with water. Cool fresh water ...

Maybe someone would find him. Maybe a ghost would appear, with a ghostly water bladder ...

Maybe ...

CHAPTER 25

# Loa

He woke to find the rubbish dog licking the wound on his leg.

For a moment he thought the animal was starting to eat him. Then he realised that she was licking him the way a mother dog licked a puppy.

He peered around, looking first for a new shape in the mud that might be a crocodile then at his wound. It looked neat and clean, not red and puffed, not nearly as long and jagged as it had seemed before. Either it had stopped bleeding by itself, or the licking had soothed it.

His knee looked worse. Purple, green. He touched it, felt pain so bad it just made him feel sick, as though his body wouldn't register so much agony. He couldn't look at it.

He looked at the rubbish dog instead.

She sat on the far side of the ledge, watching him warily. So the crocodile hasn't eaten her, he thought tiredly. Did she think he still had water bladders?

'Sorry, girl,' he said. His voice was hoarse. His lips hurt. They tasted of blood; they were dry and cracked from sun and salt. It sounded funny to talk so far from people. 'There's no water for either of us. We're meat for the crows or croc.' His voice cracked on the words, but he felt no shame: there was no one to call him a coward here.

The dog stood up. She scampered down the cliff, onto the muddy flats, then turned around, as if she was waiting for him.

Did she think he could take her back to the canoe and the water bladders?

Stupid rubbish dog. He shut his eyes again. Something rough and damp touched his arm. The dog's tongue. He opened his eyes. The rubbish dog ran down the cliff and stared at him once more.

Suddenly he understood. She wanted him to follow her.

Later he'd wonder how he knew. It had never occurred to him to follow a dog before. Had it ever occurred to anyone? But now he had nothing, no one. Just the rubbish dog.

Maybe she was taking him to be the crocodile's dinner. It didn't seem to matter now. Following a rubbish dog was the only option that he had.

CHAPTER 26

# The Dog

Why were humans so stupid?

The dog sat on her haunches and watched Bony Boy hobble along the cliff towards her. He was hurt. She understood hurt. But she could smell that he needed fresh water too.

Why didn't he let his nose guide him to water? Or at least understand when she made it quite clear that he was to follow?

But now he was following her, at least. She waited till he was closer then clambered up the rock a way, and sat, waiting till he caught up with her.

# CHAPTER 27

# Loa

The rubbish dog was taking him somewhere. He didn't know why, but he suddenly understood where.

She had found a way out of the cove.

If he hadn't been so tired, in so much pain, he might have seen the track too: a narrow passage where the rock had crumbled, leaving a rough track up between the boulders and blocks of cliff. Other animals had used the path, treading silt into packed earth bridging the gaps between the broken rocks. He could even faintly smell them — not just dog and seagulls, and not pig or human either, but animal scents he didn't recognise.

He leaned against the cliff face again to help support his weight, hopping, dragging his leg, until they reached the top. He paused, out of breath. The pain exhausted him, the storm and fright and strangeness.

He gazed around, panting. On one side the sea stretched blue and bare. On the other golden tussocks of grass spread to dull green hills in the distance, the earth between them a patchwork of cracks, parched from the sun. It looked like a land crying for water to make it live. But this was the Dry, he told himself. Rain would come to this land too.

Or would it? The land looked wrong. The colours weren't right — the green too drab, the grass too brown. Only the sea on his other side was as it should be, the bright and fearless blue. Maybe this new land never had a Rain Season to bring it back to life.

The sun glared at him, swollen as his knee. He could see the beach he'd hoped to land on from here too: a vast stretch of trackless sand. No sign of the canoe. No sign of people either. No smoke, even on the horizon.

He had tried not to think about that. It was bad being alone. No fire was worse. Now the true terror flooded over him. Fire kept the wild animals away in the night. Fire drove away the spirits of the dark. Fire warmed the body on windy nights and cooked his food.

He'd once seen his grandfather make fire by turning a dry stick in a patch of rotting wood. It had been a show-off trick. The clan always carried fire with them when they moved camp — a live coal in a slow-burning pig's tusk.

It had taken a long time for Grandfather to get the rotten wood smouldering. Could Loa even remember how it had been done?

He shut his eyes for a moment, in pain and weariness. The pain in his knee felt like knives. He needed water: soon, or he would die.

He opened his eyes. The dog was still there. 'Water?' he whispered, as though she might understand.

The rubbish dog gave a short 'hff'. She sounded impatient. She padded away, then stopped to wait for him. Loa lurched along the animal track towards her, along the cliff, then down into a sort of gorge, where two ridges met.

He stared.

There was a pond down there in the rock, almost perfectly round. Smooth cliffs surrounded it except on this side, where the path led down to it. The water was shallow, but clear. Impossible for a croc to lurk there, or even a snake.

Could it be fresh water? Or was it salt water, splashed here by some high tide?

As if to answer him the rubbish dog ran down to the pool. She drank briefly, then looked up at him as though to say, 'This is how you drink, you fool.'

'Water,' he whispered. He lumbered clumsily down the rock to the pool, then lurched into a sitting position next to the water, injured leg in front of him, and lifted up a handful.

It was warm and sweet and wonderful.

The dog gazed at him. He drank again and again, then dunked his head into the water to get rid of the salt and heat. At last he hauled himself onto his good foot again and scrambled up the path onto the rocky ridge.

He was safe from crocodiles up here. A croc could climb the path. But it wouldn't bother. The other animals that used this path, whatever they were, would be crocodile food too. Again he closed his eyes. For the first time in two days he let himself sleep without forcing down terror first.

CHAPTER 28

# Loa

He dreamed of home. His mother spilling tubers out of her bag; his father grinning as he held a fine spear against the sky. He held on to the dream even as he woke up, hoping desperately that he'd find himself on the leafy branches of a sleeping platform, the chatter of family around him.

He opened his eyes. The rock was growing chilly against his skin. The sun had sunk to the horizon. The rocks were shadowy, with vague rustlings that he didn't understand.

Back home he knew the sound of every animal. It was like he'd been dropped by an eagle far from where he should be — home, the sounds of the clan, the mutters of grandmothers, the cries of babies — to here, with just the sounds of wind and sea and strangeness.

Where was the rubbish dog? There was no sign of her — and still no smoke or canoe or people. He forced himself to lurch down to the pool again, drank, then made his way under a rocky overhang near the water. At least he'd be out of the wind down here.

He sat with his back to the rock, feeling the last of its warmth fade with the daylight. He shivered, from hunger and loneliness as much as cold.

Something warm touched his hand. For a moment he thought it was the rubbish dog's nose.

It was a bird. A dead bird, with strange red and green feathers. The dog sat next to it, looking at him.

The bird was a present for him. He picked it up. It was freshly killed, the marks of teeth where it had been choked to death.

The rubbish dog had a few feathers around her muzzle too, either from this bird or another she had eaten.

He'd eaten raw meat before, when he had been too hungry to wait for it to cook after a hunt. This wouldn't be good, but it would feed him, and not hurt him either.

He looked at it, and then at the dog. He would have died of thirst tomorrow, or died from lack of food the day after, or the day after that. The rubbish dog had given him his life.

Why?

Suddenly he began to cry. He cried like a baby, on and on, letting the tears flow and the sobs well out of him. He screamed up into the sky and felt the scream echo back. At last the sobs came quietly.

Something warm pressed against him. It was the dog. She sat next to him, her front legs poking out by his. It was almost as if they were old men sitting together.

We are, in a way, he thought. He and the dog had been through as much in the last two days as many old men had experienced in their whole lives.

The dog knew it too.

He pulled the feathers off the bird, then chewed its still faintly warm flesh. He couldn't face the guts, so the dog ate them from his fingers, licking them clean.

Then they sat together as the blanket of the night covered them, and the fruit bats made long sweeps against the sky.

CHAPTER 29

# The Dog

She waited till Bony Boy was asleep, slumped on the rock, his leg stuck out awkwardly, then padded out and along the track, up to the highest point on the cliff above them.

For a while she just sat there, letting the smells seep into her. Some were familiar, like Bony Boy, the sea, the fruit bats that flapped above the mangroves. But mostly they were strange.

There was no scent of dog at all.

At last she lifted up her nose and began to sing. It was a howl of longing, of hope. It was a song that called, 'If anyone hears this, please answer.'

But no dog did.

This new land was empty. It had no dogs at all.

She felt the moon rise out of the sea. She sat silent, then padded down to Bony Boy again.

He was all she had.

CHAPTER 30

# Loa

He slept till the sunlight washed down the cliff, dazzling him as he opened his eyes.

It was long past dawn. The tracks around the pool told him that animals had drunk and gone while he was asleep. Hunger gnawed at him, but he felt stronger after the water, the food and sleep. He sat up, glanced at his knee, then looked away again.

A shadow moved above him. It was the dog, her fur golden in the sun, lying on the rock, watching him. 'Hello,' he said.

Her head tilted to one side as though she was trying to understand. He almost grinned. He pushed himself to his feet. He needed food. He needed to explore this world.

He drank, then hopped up to the ridge again. The dog pushed her way in front of him. It seemed like she wanted to be with him too.

He gazed around. Over on the horizon, clouds lingered like round blue mountains. The air felt different: heavy and moister. The Thunder Season is coming early, he thought. That was why the storm had caught him unawares. But he felt relief too. This new land had the same seasons as the world he'd known.

Still no signs of people — no canoes, no smoke. Could a land this size really be empty?

Suddenly he felt small. Tiny. The sea went on forever ... and so did the land ... and the sky above — and he was all alone. He looked down at his body. It was a good body, for a boy his age. But was it strong enough for him to survive alone?

'Yes.' He said it aloud, even though there was only the dog to hear. She pricked up her ears, looking at him thoughtfully. 'We got here, didn't we, girl? The sea didn't get us. We'll manage.'

The dog's tail thudded on the ground. Did that mean anything?

I'm talking to a dog, he thought. And then, No. I'm talking to the animal who saved my life. All at once he knew that, no matter what, he was safe with her. He could be injured, helpless, and she wouldn't attack him. And even if he was starving, he would never see her as food again. If a crocodile attacked he'd fight for both of them.

Meanwhile they needed to eat.

He limped slowly along the path. It led to another muddy mangrove cove, bigger than the one where he'd been wrecked. The tide was low again, leaving a vast stretch of mud and trees.

He hopped down to it, the dog padding after him. His leg still hurt enough to make him giddy with pain if he tried to put all his weight on it or twisted it, and it gave way if he tried to stand on it, but if he went slowly, dragging it, lifting it where necessary, it was all right.

The raw bird hadn't even begun to satisfy his hunger. He looked at the fruit bats hanging from their roosts, at the holes in the mud that meant crabs lurked below. Fruit bat and crab were good food, but both had to be cooked.

Some foods like pandanus nuts killed you if you ate them raw. Others made you sick.

He hauled himself from tree to tree again, through the soft bubbling mud the tide had left, then used his knife to prise through half-rotted timber.

Yes! There was a mangrove worm, small and white ...

... and useless. White mangrove worms had to be cooked, or they left your throat sore and swollen. Every child had tried eating one when they were small; none ever tried it again.

He thrust the knife into another tree, then grabbed at the flash of pink and grey, laughing with delight. The giant worm dangled from his fingers to his elbow, fat and succulent. Not quite as fat as the worms would be during the Wet, but so good. He nipped off the sharp head with his teeth and spat it out, then sucked the creamy inside.

The dog made a small noise beside him.

'You want one too?'

'Gff,' said the dog.

He laughed again, and threw her the rest of the worm. She leaped up and grabbed it out of the air, then chewed it thoroughly, swallowing finally as though she had decided it was good.

He lurched over to another tree, and another, digging and feasting and throwing worms to the dog till he was full. The dog looked satisfied too.

He looked at his hands, covered in worm juice.

Babies' food. Women's food. Men hunted pigs. They speared giant rats or fish. They didn't gather worms that any toddler could find.

What were they doing back at the camp? Had Leki told them he was leaving? Or was she so rapt in Bu that she never even noticed Loa was gone?

For the first time he was glad that there was no one to see him. Not Loa the pig hunter, but Loa the cripple, digging mangrove worms.

He needed fire.

If he had fire he'd be a man again. He could eat cooked fruit bat. Arrowroot plants grew where the water seeped from the rocks. Their tubers would be sour and stringy at this time of year, but better than nothing. But they too needed to be cooked, like fruit bat.

He limped back up the track, trying to work out what he needed most. Fire first, and wood and tinder to make it. Then the right sort of rock and wood to make a spear. Fire would give him hot sand to straighten the spear shaft, but the rock here was crumbly. It would never pierce an animal's hide — it probably wouldn't even spear a fish, which he couldn't do anyway till his leg was better.

The path wasn't as steep down to the grasslands. He took his time, hauling down dead bits of branch as he walked, the crumbliest, driest wood he could find, then two long hard sticks. At last he sat, the tinder in a small pile next to him, and pressed the hard stick onto the long rotten one.

This was how Grandfather had done it, wasn't it?

The dog watched from a rock nearby, curious at first. Eventually she shut her eyes, though her ears stayed pricked.

Loa began to rub the vertical stick between his palms. Patience, he thought. It had taken Grandfather a long time to get the tinder smouldering so he could blow in it to produce flame. Rolling and rolling the stick into the rotten wood ...

The sun shone above him, hot and white. How long had he been rolling the stick? Far longer than Grandfather. He touched a finger to the tinder.

It wasn't even warm.

He let the sticks fall. It wasn't going to work. Not unless he could remember some other trick Grandfather used to make a spark.

He glanced up at the dog. She snapped lazily at a passing fly and crunched it.

Not a fly. A bee!

He sat perfectly still and listened. There was no telltale hum from any of the nearby trees. He watched the air instead, till he found another bee, then blinked.

The bee had vanished into the ground!

Bees lived in trees back home. But he was sure that had been a bee.

He grabbed one of the sticks he'd hoped to use as firewood, and used it to help him limp over to the tiny hole in the ground. He put his head down to the soil and listened.

A hive!

He grinned. He poked the stick into the hole, making it bigger and bigger still. The bees poured out. He brushed them away, glad that bees couldn't sting like biting flies, then bent down and scooped out two handfuls of honey and wax.

It was wonderful, though not as sweet as the honey he'd known before. This was runnier and slightly green-tinged. He ate handful after handful, spitting out the wax onto a little mound that grew as he ate.

A shadow sat next to him. The dog. He held out a hand, sticky with honey.

The dog licked it, blinked, licked again, then gave an almost-grin of distaste. It was so funny he had to laugh.

At last he gathered the wax and stood up. The wax had given him an idea. He mightn't have a spear point, but he had his knife. He could use wax and twine to fasten it to a long stick.

It wouldn't be a proper spear, not balanced enough to hunt with, not until he could straighten the stick with hot wet sand. But it would be good enough to spear fish. He could stand still on the rocks at the edge of the sandy beach he'd tried to land on and let the fish come to him, then strike. His bad leg wouldn't matter. You could eat fish raw if you had to.

And he'd be a hunter. A man.

CHAPTER 31

# The Dog

## The Thunder Season

Days passed. The smells here were strange, and many of the animals and birds too, but at least day and night and Bony Boy were still the same.

Bony Boy was a boring companion. He moved slowly and awkwardly. Most dawns she left him to hunt alone, following strange scents for the fun of it, for Bony Boy found enough food for both of them now.

This morning she lay on her tummy in the grasslands, the dry grass the same colour as her fur. Slowly the world around her woke up, the birds singing, then rising in a shifting cloud to settle on the grass nearby.

She moved slowly, still on her tummy, closer, closer. One of the birds saw her and gave a warning cry. The cloud rose again, just as she leaped at the closest bird.

Snap! She'd only caught its wing, but that was enough to stop it flying. She dropped it onto the grass, then picked it up properly, still squirming, broke its neck and took it up onto the ridge to eat.

She could smell the world there; she followed Bony Boy's scent as he woke up and drank then headed down to the rocks at the edge of the headland with his new long stick. She chewed the bird slowly, spitting out the feathers, then let herself doze.

There was no hurry. It would take Bony Boy a while to spear a fish. He never ate the fish meat straight away, but cut it into pieces and left it on the hot rock with slices of fruit over it.

She didn't like the fruit-covered pieces. They were soft and tasted wrong. But he always left the head and tail for her; and the fish guts too.

There was time to sleep in the sun now.

## CHAPTER 32

# Loa

Loa stood on the rock and peered into the water. He wished he could fish properly, striding into the waves, but his knee still gave way under him if he tried to walk with the splints off. But if he was patient most days he could spear a fish here on the rocks. He had made fish hooks too, 'finding' the hooks hidden in the shells on the beach.

The new spear didn't fly straight, but he was used to that now. He'd cut a hole in the end and tied cord to it and his waist so he didn't lose it in the waves. His obsidian knife point was the most precious thing in his world.

A fish glinted in the water, almost near enough, but not quite. He waited. One fish usually meant more.

Then there they were, twisting and cutting their way through the wave. He aimed and cast quickly, laughing with joy as the water turned bloody.

He'd got one!

I am the best hunter in the world, he thought. His smile vanished. He was the only hunter in this world.

He hauled in the spear and fish. The fish was as long as his arm and still flapping, so he bashed its head against the rock, then examined his spear. The point was still secure, he saw thankfully. It had taken days to get it right — he didn't want to have to do it again soon.

He carried the fish along the beach then up the track to the cliff top by the pool. He'd seen crocodile tracks on the beach, though he hadn't seen a croc since the one in the cove. But crocs were cunning, lying so still, so mud-covered, that you thought they were a log until it was too late.

The fruit were where he'd left them: small, sour mangrove berries. Later in the year they'd be fatter and sweeter, but when he sliced them and laid them on top of slices of fish on the hot rock in the sun like the women did at home the berry juice and the heat turned the fish flesh white and cooked.

Women's work, he thought bitterly. Collecting fruit, slicing fish. No wonder Leki had chosen Bu. Loa was a cripple, a fool who had lost his way, who lived like a woman with a rubbish dog in a bare barren land.

He gazed out at his new world. Dry grass, limp trees, smoke ...

He stilled. Smoke! It was almost at the horizon, but there was no mistaking it for cloud. A high plume of smoke, the sort of fire you'd build for a feast, a gathering of clans.

A campfire! He felt the grin spread across his face. Other people. Aunties who might know how to heal his leg, girls ...

He stopped smiling.

Hunters who'd look at him with scorn — a lost boy with a bad leg. But maybe his leg would keep getting better. And even living as a cripple with a clan would be better than trying to survive alone on raw fish and mangrove worms.

He looked around for the dog. She usually came down to him about now. 'Dog!' he yelled.

No sign of her. For a moment he hesitated. He didn't want to leave her behind. The dog was all he had.

But he was a hunter! What hunter would wait for a dog instead of striding out to find others of his kind? And if he waited the fire might go out and the smoke vanish.

He couldn't stride, but he could limp. And anyway, the dog would find his tracks and follow, he told himself. She'd sniff out the way he'd gone just like he'd watched her sniff out tiny rock lizards, crunching them in her sharp teeth.

He forced himself to eat the still-raw fish, then drank as much as he could, wishing he had water bladders. The smoke was inland and he had no way to carry water.

But there must be streams here, even in the Dry. And the smoke was less than a day's walk away. He could manage — just — to get there and back to here without water.

He hoped he didn't have to.

CHAPTER 33

# Loa

The sun had risen high behind him when the dog bounded up a few handspans later. He'd been walking for long enough to have worried she wouldn't come. She ran to him. She sniffed his feet, then lay on her back so he could bend down and scratch her tummy, something he'd discovered she liked in the long afternoons when hunger and thirst were sated and there was nothing else to do. He grinned at her, relieved she'd finally found him.

He stood up, leaning on his spear, and peered across the dry tussocks at the smoke again. The smoke cloud was bigger than it had been. The smoke was black as well as white too.

The fire was coming closer.

Suddenly he realised what it meant. That wasn't a tame campfire. This was wildfire! Fire lit by lightning crashing into the ground, perhaps, though he hadn't seen a lightning storm in all the days since he'd been here.

Maybe there'd been a storm in the distance, when he had been sleeping. He'd lost track of time and this land had few of the season's cues he was used to, though he was sure the seasons were the same as at home. Storms could come at any time now that the year had turned.

The fire might also have been lit by people to flush out animals to spear. In any case, its cause didn't matter. The fire was heading for him and the dog.

He had no way to know how fierce it was. Wildfire could be a frog fire, jumping and snickering through the grass, so you were safe in a tree — if you could hold your breath till the worst of the smoke passed. Or it could be a monster fire that ate trees too. Suddenly the fire was an enemy, not a friend. Only one thing stopped fire.

Water.

The sea was too far behind him. But over to the south-west was a grey-green smudge that must be an inland mangrove swamp, perhaps by a river or lake. The ground would be too wet to burn there. It would stop a frog fire, but not a monster. A monster fire would eat the swamp trees too, leaving the land dried and scarred.

But the swamp was the only refuge he had.

He turned abruptly, and began to limp as fast as he could, not worrying now about hurting his leg more. Legs could heal ... perhaps. Burned bodies didn't. The dog bounced at his heels or 'followed him in front': she had a way of knowing where he was going and heading there first.

He looked behind. The smoke was a wide tear across the world now, the wind at its back. But the swamp was close. He lurched into its dampness just as he heard the first snicker of flames behind him. He waited till he was several spear lengths in among the trees, balancing on a root clump with the water pooled about his feet, staining the dog's paws, then turned back again to look at the fire.

The flames licked up at the sky. The blaze was bigger than a frog fire, but not much. The red flames bit and frizzled at the mangrove edges. A few leaves turned into flame. But although he could feel the fire's heat he knew they were safe. Already the flames were shrinking.

More than safe. He suddenly realised that this was his chance to catch some fire for himself.

He untied his spear and thrust it safely up into a tree, then began to gather whatever dry wood and dead branches hadn't fallen into the mud. He limped with an armful over to the edge of the fire.

Most of it was already out, but the rotten wood on one of the outer mangroves still flickered red. He kneeled down as well as his bad leg would let him, and pushed the wood he had collected next to the coals, then blew on them. Flames flared up, yellow and eager. He added twigs then larger branches. When those were burning, he ventured further into the swamp and hauled out a dead log.

It was far bigger than any mangrove tree. The great tides must come all the way inland to this swamp in the Rain Season, he decided, or maybe a river flowed here too. Some past flood had washed this giant log here. The wood was damp, but that was good. It would burn more slowly and give him time to move his fire somewhere else.

He couldn't camp here. Even a big fire wouldn't keep crocodiles away. And he'd come too far to return to the seaside cliffs tonight. He climbed a tree awkwardly, using his arms to haul himself up instead of his legs, and peered around, trying to see what lay beyond the swamp.

Yes! There was a range of hills, much like the cliffs by the sea, on the other side of the mangroves. Would there be another freshwater pool there?

There was only one way to find out.

'Dog! Come on!' The dog had been watching the fire warily. She was growing fatter, Loa noticed. She must be eating well, with her own hunting and his leftovers. She ate better than any rubbish dog back home. He grinned. She could share his cooked fruit bat now.

It still hurt to think of home. The pain in his knee was nothing compared to that. Sometimes he was even glad of the injury, because it distracted him from longing for his family.

The dog leaped to her feet and followed him.

## CHAPTER 34

# Loa

Boy and dog sat by the fire under a wide rock ledge, chewing the last of the fruit bat. The meat was sweet and tender, the fur singed off before he'd roasted it in the coals, with arrowroot tubers too, and some of the white mangrove worms as well now that he could cook them. He and the dog ate till they were full, then kept on eating.

The stars lazed in a wide wheel above him, the tiny campfires of the sky. Thunder boomed far off past the grasslands. But it didn't matter now if a storm flashed across the land, not with the ledge to shelter him. Not with the fire to keep him warm.

The fire was more than warmth, more than good meals to come. Fire was a way of saying to the darkness, 'I am here, I command this tiny place where my light will keep you at bay.'

It was a way to say to wild dogs, even to crocodiles, 'You may be able to eat me, but I command fire. Watch out.'

The ledge was halfway up the first hill, worn away by wind and rain, strong and big enough to shelter him from the rains that would come soon, deep enough to even protect him from the worst of the wind. The floor was uneven, but he could fix that tomorrow, scraping dirt down to make it more comfortable.

He'd found no rockpool, but there was a tiny spring at the base of the hill, enough to gather handfuls of water and for the dog to lap. If it had been the beginning of the Dry he'd have worried that it would vanish. But the Rain would be here soon enough to replenish it.

Even better, there was food all around. This swamp was even richer than the one by the sea. He could bake swamp oysters and crabs. There were pandanus trees too, still with nuts he could now cook. He could use the leaves to make fibre for nets and cord too.

But best was the fire. He'd made a rough basket of pandanus leaves to carry the hot coals from his first fire. It had taken four attempts to get them to his new camp. The first coals had eaten through the basket and his next two efforts had gone out. But now he had a fire where he needed it. He dragged up a damp log that would burn slowly so the coals would keep glowing overnight.

Tomorrow he'd find more logs, spear more fruit bats. He could sit quite still, like the dog, and catch the lizards that ran about the rocks. She crunched them raw, but he could cook his now.

Despite his loneliness he laughed. Food, shelter, warmth, the dog — life was ...

... no, not good. But better.

## CHAPTER 35

# The Dog

It was good to have a camp with fire and meat and bones. Camp life was familiar for a rubbish dog. Bony Boy caught more food too.

She needed food, especially now. Something different was happening to her. She didn't know quite what it was, but she knew what she needed.

She ate and ate.

Each night when Bony Boy slept she left his fire and hunted in the darkness, finding her way by smell, not sight. At last she found it — a crevice, deep in the rock. A place where a dog might hide in safety, where even Bony Boy would never look. It was too small for the big lizards to get into, too deep for hawks or eagles, too high for crocodiles.

She waited. She ate; she hunted with Bony Boy.

Then one morning she knew the time had come.

She walked slowly up to the crevice, crept on her tummy into the darkness and lay down to wait.

CHAPTER 36

# Loa

Clouds gathered like clustered islands on the horizon every day now. Rain scattered across the grasslands — not the proper rain of the Wet, but enough to bring pale green shoots of grass through the cracked dry plains. Thunder growled behind winds that shifted back and forth, bringing long birds that strode through the new grasslands.

The land changed. Great tides turned the swamp into a small sea twice a day, retreating to leave driftwood, new banks of mud and sand, and giant shellfish or tiny cone shells to be roasted on the coals, the flesh within sea-sweet and tangy.

His knee was healing. Too slowly — he wanted to be able to run and leap and climb properly again. But he could put weight on it now, though he still needed to keep it bound, as any twisting made it swell.

He was hauling more driftwood up to the fire when he saw a creature move out of the corner of his eye.

He dropped the bundle of wood in shock. It was — impossible!

The creature was the size of a person and on two legs so at first he wondered if it *was* human: if this peculiar new land had people with tails. The animal's feet were huge, its head small, its ears cocked up like the dog's. The creature saw him, blinked, then bounded off ...

It was leaping, not running. He stared at it as it vanished behind a cliff. Had he imagined it?

He tried to picture the creature again. Was it dangerous? No. Its eyes were close together, like a grass eater's, not on either side of its head like a meat eater's, like a man's or a pig's or an eagle's. This animal was to be hunted, not a hunter.

But what kind of animal hopped?

Where was the dog? If the dog could see the creature, chased it, he'd know it was real. But where was she? He realised he hadn't seen her since the night before.

He was used to waking up to find her gone, but she always came back sometime during the day, nosing curiously at whatever he'd caught to eat.

'Dog! Here, girl!'

No dog appeared. Loa began to pick up the fallen wood.

She'd be back.

The dog wasn't back by dusk.

He sat by the fire, piled high with wood to make a good blaze, for comfort rather than warmth. He'd raked some of the coals away to cook a giant water snake he'd found caught in the newly lush swamp, grabbing its neck before it could strike him and lashing it down hard to break its back.

He didn't think the big snake was poisonous, not like the thin deadly sea snakes, but he was going to cook it well anyway. The aunties said that long cooking made a snake safe.

What would the aunties be doing now? It was almost as though they were no longer real. But somewhere the camp went on, with its high sleeping platforms, its laughter and friendships.

The loss of his clan hurt like a wound. He missed friends the most — other hunters to share his world with. He only had a dog.

But where was she?

He looked out into the darkness, hoping to hear her claws on the rock, or at least her howl in the distance. There was plenty of snake meat for both of them — lots of bones for a rubbish dog to chew for days.

But no dog appeared out of the darkness now. He was really alone.

# CHAPTER 37

# Loa

The dog didn't appear the next day, or the one after that either. More of the strange hopping animals arrived, big ones like the one he had seen first and small ones. He studied them with a hunter's eyes. They stood still and vulnerable as they ate the newly shooting grass. They looked like good meat — hunter's meat. But they moved quickly whenever he was near. He'd need two good legs if he was to get close. He suspected it might need more than one hunter to get close enough to spear one too.

Once again he searched for the dog, calling, though in his heart he knew there was no use.

So much could happen to a rubbish dog. A crocodile could take one — he'd seen croc tracks by their new camp too: at least one big one and a few smaller. She might have been bitten by a snake. If either had happened there was little chance of finding the dog alive.

He missed her. It wasn't just that she was familiar — nor just that she'd saved his life. Somehow, in the past few weeks, the dog had become a sort of person. Independent, intelligent, quietly companionable — the sort you'd want for a friend, whether they had two legs or four.

Now she was gone.

He sat by the campfire, the bones and scraps he hadn't wanted to eat making a smelly pile that attracted the flies. He hadn't known it was possible to feel this alone.

At last he banked down the fire with a couple of damp swamp logs that would smoulder till dawn. He lay down on the smoothed dirt, the stones now raked away, the rock behind him warmed by the fire. Once again thunder muttered in the distance.

It would rain before morning. He shut his eyes and slept.

He woke to the sight of a gold shadow at the corner of his camp, nosing at the pile of scraps. He yelled and sat up. 'Dog!'

He grabbed his spear to help himself to his feet. The dog grabbed a hunk of cooked snake and sprang from the ledge. He watched her scramble down the hill and vanish into the rocks and trees beyond.

What was wrong with her? Had he offended her? No — you couldn't offend a rubbish dog! It was like saying you could insult a pig or a cuscus.

Was she suddenly scared of him? Why would she be? He hadn't done anything new or different. She had watched him use his new spear for days without fear; she'd known that spearing animals meant food for her.

And yet she'd gone.

He sat to think about it. He knew more about pigs than rubbish dogs. Why bother studying rubbish dogs? Rubbish dogs were just ... there. They cleaned up the scraps; they were good for food if there was nothing else; and they helped little boys play at being hunters.

Had she found a pack of dogs to join? He hadn't heard any dog howls, except for hers. If any dog had heard her it would have howled back, unless the dogs here were silent.

No. He'd have seen a pack's tracks. There had been many strange tracks, but only one set of dog paw prints — hers.

Where had she gone?

He'd wait, he decided. She obviously still wanted his leftovers. He'd bring back a couple of fruit bats as soon as it was light — she loved the crunch of their brittle bones.

He was a hunter, wasn't he? Even with a bad knee he could track a dog.

He'd be waiting when she came again.

## CHAPTER 38

# Loa

She came at dusk, a shadow among shadows. The air greyed around her. Somehow she had become a grey dog; the sunlight-gold of her coat had seeped away with the daylight.

She didn't look at him, though she must have known he was there. It was almost as though she thought that if she didn't look at him directly, he couldn't see her.

He waited till she'd slipped down the hill, then followed her. There was just enough light to see her track. He could smell where she'd been too — not just her doggy scent but the ripe fruit smell of cooked bat. The trail led upwards again, then stopped.

He peered into the growing darkness. There was a deeper slash of dark in the rock. A crevice.

She must be there. Hiding.

From him?

It was too late to see into the crevice now, to see if she was really there and why she was hiding.

Tomorrow, he thought, as he limped back up to the campfire, a red blaze throwing shadows into the night. I will find out her secret tomorrow.

CHAPTER 39

# Loa

It rained heavily during the night and cleared just before dawn. Morning light speared through the thinning mist. The sun had lost its brilliant whiteness now that the sky held clouds again.

Yesterday's leftovers were already flyblown. He'd hunt and eat later.

Below him the hoppers bent their delicate heads to the grass. Overnight the world had become green, grass green, mangrove green. Even the trees were freshly washed. He could almost see the hoppers getting fatter.

He limped down to the spring, using his spear as a crutch, and found that it had become a creek meandering towards the swamp. It even tasted different: of leaves and growing things, not its old tinny taste of rock and earth.

Something moved on the hill above. The dog. He stilled as she slunk past. She must have smelled him and chosen to ignore him. He waited till she crept up towards the leftovers, then circled around up to her crevice and peered in.

It took a moment for his eyes to adjust to the

dimness and see them. Puppies. Five tiny squirming bundles with their eyes sealed shut. So *that* was why ...

Something growled behind him.

He froze, remembering the sow's fury when humans had threatened her piglets.

The dog had been his companion since the storm. But he knew that a mother dog would let nothing — not even him — threaten her puppies. He tried to breathe thinly, shallowly, as though he wasn't breathing at all. He looked away, not at her, not at the crevice where the puppies wriggled. He pushed himself back from the opening, not getting up to his feet, but sliding along the rock. It was only when he was a spear's length away that he allowed himself to look at her.

She carried a piece of cooked fruit bat. It must be for herself — he supposed rubbish dogs' puppies lived on milk when they were very small, like most other animals.

She met his eyes. She growled again — an almost imperceptible sound, like the rock had vibrated. She was waiting for him to leave before she went in to her pups. But he couldn't go any higher, not with his bad leg. He'd have to go past her to get down.

He sat there, hardly breathing, wondering if she would drop the meat and go for him. But at last she lowered to her stomach and wriggled into the crevice.

He let out his breath. Heart pounding, he limped down the path, careful not to linger by the crevice in case she jumped out at him. He made his way to the edge of the swamp, quickly speared a sleeping fruit bat — they never seemed to realise that one of their number was gone when they woke at night — then carried it back up to his fire.

He sat as it roasted, looking out at the new green of the grasslands.

What would the dog do now? Would she ever come back to him? Or would the puppies be her pack now? Dogs stayed with dogs, humans with humans. That was the way the world was. It should be as impossible as having a whale as a friend. And yet, he thought, we have been friends. It was not just an alliance of convenience.

Could he bear the loneliness if she left for good?

He pulled at the fruit bat's wing to see if it was cooked enough; the bone slid out. He tore off the wing with two bits of twig so he didn't burn himself, waited till it had cooled a bit and began to chew. Suddenly he longed for real meat — not shellfish or mangrove worm or bat. Hunter's meat. There were no pigs, but one of the hopping animals would do.

He needed to find other people. He hadn't seen any more smoke in the distance, but that didn't mean there was no one there. Perhaps they made small hot fires with little smoke. Most of his clan's fires were like that: dry driftwood that flared hot and almost smokeless.

He could even try to get back home. Not in a canoe — even if he'd had an adze, or a rock that could be made into an adze head, he knew he didn't have enough skill to make a canoe that would take him that far. A canoe looked simple, but it had to be perfectly balanced or it rolled over. He'd need years of learning and practice to manage that.

But he *could* make a raft, the logs tied together with cord made from twisted inner bark, waterproofed with flame. A raft would take him ...

Not home, he realised. The winds and current had brought him here. Now they'd take him even further away. He couldn't paddle against them, especially not on a clumsy raft. But if he went further along the coast he might see campfire smoke.

Perhaps.

He sagged against the rock. The Rain Season was nearly upon him, with its drenching showers and then its wild storms. If he was caught in a storm now there'd be no sandbank to rescue him. The first giant wave would smash him into the sea.

The Rain Season meant floods too. He didn't know this land and how strong the floods and storms might be. At least he was pretty sure he was out of the water's reach up here — there was no debris among the rocks or in the trees. But once he ventured down onto the grasslands a flood might cut him off from the safety of cliffs and high country, easy meat for crocodiles.

No, he had to stay here till after the Wet. Alone.

He came to a decision. The dog had trusted him before. He'd win her back. He'd bring her meat ... He grinned at himself. Like a warrior courting a girl he wanted for his wife. There were no girls to win here, but he could try to persuade a dog to be his friend.

## CHAPTER 40

# The Dog

It was hard, living by herself. Not the puppies — that had been easy enough, each in its little membrane sac that she'd chewed up so no predator would smell it. She liked the feel of them feeding. Liked the smell of them, that familiar scent of puppy and dog.

It was good not to be the only dog again.

It was food that was so difficult — and dangerous too. Back in the pack the uncles brought the mothers and puppies food. That way the mothers didn't have to leave the puppies alone and vulnerable to hunt.

The uncles sniffed out danger: few predators would attack a pack of dogs. But there were no uncles here.

She had sniffed out danger here herself, though she wasn't sure what it was — the scent was unfamiliar. But it smelled like a meat eater.

She thought it had smelled her too. And her puppies.

At least she didn't have to spend much time away: just long enough to get to Bony Boy's camp and back. But there were so many things that would gladly kill a small, blind, helpless puppy. Snakes and hawks, to start with. The babies could even just crawl out and fall off the ledge.

She hated being away, but there was no choice. Instinct told her she had to eat so she could feed her pups. She was hungry again now, but she hesitated, sniffing the air as she poked her head out of the crevice, checking to see if she could smell danger before she slunk away.

She stopped. The hair on her neck rose. There *was* another scent. Bony Boy! She pulled herself back into the crevice just as he limped up the path; she let out a low, rumbling growl.

Humans ate dogs. The almost forgotten fear was back. She wasn't going to let a hunter have her babies.

Bony Boy stopped. Had he heard her growl? Something clattered against the entrance of the crevice. A spear?

And then she smelled it. Meat. Freshly cooked too. Half a fruit bat, still with the innards that were the bit she liked best.

She pulled it inside hurriedly, then peered out again. Bony Boy sat a little way up the path. He didn't move.

Not hunting, she thought. He had brought her food ... just like an uncle dog did.

The sense of threat faded a little. She still wouldn't leave her puppies while he was here, even to get a drink. But at least now she had meat. She chewed the bones while her puppies suckled.

And all the while Bony Boy just sat there, in the sun.

CHAPTER 41

# Loa

He brought food to the dog every morning. At first she grabbed it, not looking at him directly, and dragged it inside. But today she sat in the sunlight near him, eating, like before.

It gave him a good feeling, providing food for the dog and her puppies. It was a bit like a hunter bringing home meat for the camp.

He plucked a fruit bat out of the tree first thing each morning now, as soon as he knew they'd be safely asleep. He'd tried cooking two, leaving one to take her the next day. But something had stolen the cold fruit bat when he left the camp briefly to get a drink.

Had a buzzard taken it? An eagle? There were many tracks in the dirt here, but none on the hard rock around his ledge.

It didn't matter. One fruit bat a day was enough for himself and the dog. That way there were no leftovers to attract scavengers.

He lay back against the warm stone, almost dozing. Peace seeped through him. The dog, her puppies, the flicker of his fire glowing beyond them on the hill.

Above him the thunderclouds slowly gathered in the sky.

CHAPTER 42

# The Dog

She needed to drink. She'd snuck out before dawn to drink, but now the puppies needed more milk she needed to drink more often too.

She stared at Bony Boy, leaning against the cliff. Sometime in the last few days she had almost accepted he wasn't a threat to her pups.

Almost. Not quite. If he made any move towards them she'd savage him.

But he brought her food. He sat by the crevice, like an uncle, even if he didn't smell like one.

She sniffed the air again. The danger scent was still there. But she needed water. The puppies needed her milk. And Bony Boy was here.

She stood up and slunk quietly down towards the stream.

CHAPTER 43

# Loa

He watched the dog trot down the path.

She needs a drink, he thought.

He waited till she was out of sight, then leaned down to peer into the crevice. He didn't dare get nearer — he knew she'd smell where he had been.

He could just see the puppies. They had grown even in the past few days: plump balls of fur tumbling over each other. One was even nosing out towards the opening, looking for its mother.

He grinned. They were so small, so ... doggy.

Something moved behind him. He turned, just in time.

A talon lashed at him. Mottled yellow-grey jaws and claws longer than a spearhead. He flung himself back, grabbed his spear, then held it out, his back safe against the wall.

The beast stared at him. It was a lizard. He'd seen others a bit like it — but they'd been no bigger than his hand. This was a giant. It was wider than his thighs and taller than he was as it reared up, a couple of spear lengths away, striking again with its claws.

He thrust his spear out to frighten it, then realised

that the clawing was a threat too, designed to frighten *him* away. It wasn't after him.

The lizard beast wanted the puppies.

It had been waiting till the dog left. Why bother fighting when you could gulp down puppies and vanish back up the rock?

The monster lowered itself onto its four lizard legs and peered into the crevice.

Loa strode forwards, ignoring the pain in his leg. He thrust his spear deep into the reptile's belly.

The lizard reared back, twisting and trying to bite at the pain. Loa's spear snapped in his hand.

He stared at the monster as it hissed. A single fierce spear thrust hadn't been enough to kill it, though it might die of the wound later. But now ...

Now the giant lizard had his knife in its guts, his precious knife. It could still grab the puppies. It could still ...

The reptile reared once more, blood dripping from its wound. A talon slashed at Loa.

This time it wasn't trying to frighten him. This time it meant to kill.

His spear was only a stick now. A stick was better than no weapon at all. He aimed it at the tiny lizard eyes.

The stick caught it a heavy blow on the nose instead. The lizard retreated and then struck again. Loa aimed at the throat this time. The stick didn't break the skin, but it was enough to stop the determined lunge. He tried not to think of those massive claws raking his body.

The monster hissed again, showing its long narrow tongue. It reared above him, closer now. He waited for the claws to strike.

All at once it turned. He used the moment and struck again, harder, closer, into the vulnerable skin of its stomach.

The monster lizard dropped back onto its belly. His stick broke again, leaving him with little more than half an arm's length of wood. Loa saw the dog, her teeth clamped on the lizard's tail.

She leaped at the monster's throat. She gripped and tore at the flesh as Loa too struck again and again. The monster lizard clawed at them, waving its legs one way and then another. But each time it turned either Loa or the dog lunged deeper into its flesh.

He didn't know how long they fought, but suddenly it was over. There was just the monster, sprawled limply on its back, bleeding from stomach and neck. The dog, with a bloody muzzle but unhurt; the puppies cowering far back in the dimness of the crevice. He counted them — still five — then looked at himself.

Blood on his legs, his arms. He wiped it gingerly, then realised it was the lizard's blood, not his.

The dog lay on her front, panting. She stood up slowly, then moved towards the lizard's stomach. She was going to feed.

'No!' Loa stepped towards her without thinking. For a second he thought the dog was going to attack him — this was her kill too and her blood lust was up. Then all at once she dropped to her belly again.

He reached his hand carefully into the hole in the lizard's stomach. He needed to find his precious knife.

It was still attached to the first bit of spear. He yanked the wood out, his hand even bloodier, then used the knife to hack off some meat from one of the hind legs, and along the backbone, always the best bits on any large animal.

Tonight he'd eat meat. Real meat, hunter's meat — not fruit bat.

He was almost back at his camp before he realised that he and the dog had fought together.

## CHAPTER 44

# Loa

Loa hauled another log onto the stack under his overhang, glad that his knee was nearly better now. The wood should stay dry there. He'd moved the fire under shelter too. The overhang was smoky now, but that was better than letting his precious fire go out, plus the smoke kept away the mosquitoes that swarmed up in great clouds these days.

It rained most days now: not the heavy deluges of the Rain Season proper, but the regular rains of the Thunder time. The way back to the sea was cut off by rising swamp waters. Part of the grasslands had turned to swamp too. The mangrove forest that had saved him from the fire was a swiftly flowing stream. Fish lay wriggling in the tussocks after every new storm brought a quick rise and fall of flood water.

He feasted on fish and crab. The figs were sweet and ripe now too, as well as a black fruit. He'd tried only a taste of them first, then a little more when they didn't make him sick. He still limited himself to a few a day, as a change from the figs.

The dog ate the leftover fish, but there were no fruit bats to give her now. Either they'd finally realised he was attacking them as they slept and moved their roosting spot, or they always moved camp at this time of year.

He knew the dog hunted lizards and frogs and birds to feed her puppies. There'd been no more monster lizards — though at least that one had given her all the meat she could eat for days. When he'd arrived the next day she'd hauled the carcass away from her crevice. He supposed that was so it didn't attract other meat eaters that might then be tempted by her puppies.

Something moved behind him. A pair of hoppers: the small ones, not the big ones taller than he was. The grass was long now from the rains. He'd noticed that the big hoppers only ate grass while the small ones ate leaves and shrubs too.

His spear was better now he had been able to straighten the new shaft in hot sand, but the hoppers still never came close enough for him to spear them. He'd tried sneaking up, or even standing still, leaves about his waist, his legs together, looking down to hide his eyes, all the hunting tricks to disguise himself as he waited for them to come and graze. But they seemed to be able to scent him long before he was close enough to harm them, even if he covered himself in swamp mud and approached them from downwind.

It's like pig hunting, he thought. Pigs were wily. You needed another hunter or, better still, many men, to drive the pigs towards the spears. Or luck, he acknowledged, grinning at the memory of that last pig hunt.

Would he ever hunt pig again? Ever get home, or even find other people? There was no way to even attempt it now until the next Dry.

What was his clan doing now? Did his mother still hope he'd return after the rains, bringing a bride with him? Or had Leki even forgotten she'd spoken to him in the excitement of marrying Bu? Perhaps she had left with Bu before he'd been missed. His family might think he had been eaten by a shark, or taken by a crocodile. Perhaps they'd searched for him.

He shut his eyes for a moment. He hoped they weren't still searching. But deep down he knew his mother would always scan the horizon for her son's canoe. Every time his father tracked game in the forest he'd look for a print that might be Loa's.

But there was no way to tell them he was safe.

He shivered. He needed to *do* something. He'd collected enough food and wood, which left him with the rest of the day to fill.

At least he had the puppies to watch now. He picked up the second fish he'd caught at dawn and limped down the track then up again to the dog's crevice. He sat on a rock just below it, out of the mud — he'd noticed that the dog always had to sit higher than him. Her nose appeared as she caught wind of him and the food.

He put the fish down. She crawled out on her belly, grabbed it, then dragged it slightly uphill. The puppies followed.

Their eyes had opened now. They were fat-bellied and fuzzy, with gold fur like her. He had a sudden memory of eating roast puppy last year, but thrust it away.

The puppies tumbled about the dog as she ate. Finally she stopped and let them drink, then gave a short cough. Regurgitated fish, and what might have been bird too, landed on the rock. The puppies began to eat, their tiny tails wagging. The dog watched them. Loa did too. It was fascinating to see the puppies grow. He'd watched animals and birds and fish all his life, but only as food.

At last the puppies finished eating. The dog lay back. She seemed to be sleeping in the sun, but her ears were still pricked.

One of the puppies lifted his tiny nose. He was the smallest one, a boy Loa had named Little. He sat for a second, thinking, then trotted down the path.

Loa froze. Was he coming to him?

He was too small to be a danger, of course — those tiny teeth would be mere thorn pricks. But what if the dog thought he might hurt her puppy?

Little had reached him now. Loa sat perfectly still as the puppy sniffed his hands — the fish smell, he supposed — and then his feet and bottom and then his hands again. The tiny whiskers tickled.

'Hff,' Little said. And climbed onto his lap.

Loa glanced at the dog, trying not to move at all. The dog raised her head. She stared at him, then at the puppy on his lap.

Did the puppy think he was a warm rock? Maybe Little liked sitting on the highest point around, just like the dog did?

'Hff,' said the puppy again. He wasn't trying to eat him. It was ... almost ... as if he was trying to play.

Loa reached out his hand cautiously, still glancing at the dog. But even as he looked she put her head back down on her paws. Had she given him permission to touch her puppy? He stroked one finger down the puppy's back. He had felt dog fur many times, but until the dog had allowed him to rub her stomach it had only been when the dog was dead. Puppy fur seemed softer. The puppy rolled over, wriggling with delight.

Another puppy approached, a girl this time. He helped her scramble onto his lap.

The dog lay still, listening, watching.

'Ow!' Tiny, needle-sharp teeth bit into his finger. 'No!' he said, tapping her nose automatically.

The puppy grunted. Loa flashed another look at the dog. But it seemed she was even happy to have him discipline the pups too. Like a human with a baby, he thought. Did dogs teach their puppies not to bite each other, to share food and how to hunt?

He grinned as the puppies tried to grab his fingers again. He was going to find out!

CHAPTER 45

# The Dog

She watched her puppies play with Bony Boy. Somehow he wasn't just Bony Boy now. He was the man-uncle who brought food, helped guard the den, who played with the puppies and nipped them if they bit too hard. The world was almost right again.

She was hungry though. Fish filled her belly, but she wanted meat. She sniffed the air. There was food down there, hopping through the grass. They were fast, those hoppers. She'd tried to catch them before. A pack of dogs takes it in turn to chase their prey, turning around in wide circles till they were tired, then a fresh dog could leap out and grab one for the pack to eat. One dog alone couldn't hunt like that.

But she wasn't alone any more.

She got to her feet, stretched, checked her puppies were safe with Bony Boy, then padded down the path.

CHAPTER 46

# Loa

'No,' said Loa firmly, as the puppy tried to tear the fish from his fingers. He held the flesh up in the air as the puppy leaped up, trying to grab it.

Little Boy's puppy teeth were sharp. If the pup got into the habit of grabbing food from him now, he might keep doing it when he was fully grown and dangerous.

The puppy leaped again.

'Down!' said Loa.

He grinned at himself. Last year he'd have laughed if anyone had told him watching rubbish dogs could be fascinating.

The puppy sat on his furry bottom, his head on one side. Suddenly he rolled over. He looked up at him, so small and fluffy and silly Loa couldn't help but scratch his tummy, then give him a bit of his fish.

The puppy sat up and gulped it down, then looked at him consideringly. He rolled over again, looking hopeful.

'You think you'll get more fish if you roll over for me, do you?' said Loa.

'Grrff,' said the puppy.

'Well, you're right.' He let the puppy lick the last of the fish from his fingers, as the one he'd named Little Girl padded up. She sat and looked at him, then rolled over too.

Loa laughed. These pups were clever! 'No more fish. All gone, see?' Loa held up his empty hands. Little Girl sat up again and whined.

He grinned again. 'All right, here you are.'

He tugged a piece of smoked fish from his belt. He kept a small store now, in case a storm stopped him hunting. The puppy tugged at it eagerly. Loa pulled off another piece when Little Boy rolled over again too.

The other three puppies tugged at the skeleton of the fish a little way away. Those three never approached him, though they didn't seem scared of him.

He looked at Little Boy and Little Girl, still chewing at the leathery smoked fish. They were so small, so ... silly. That was it. They made you feel good just watching them wriggle and pounce as he dangled his fingers near them ...

Suddenly a bird gave an alarm call down below. Loa looked up, searching the clearing. The hoppers were moving, three or four of them bounding towards his camp through the long grass.

Crocodile? He hadn't seen any packs here yet, but crocs could travel far and fast at this time of year. Another monster lizard? He grabbed his spear, tumbling the puppies from his lap. They scampered up to their crevice. The other three had already vanished, as though they too sensed danger below.

The hoppers still bounded straight towards him, as though instinctively seeking the rocks and crevices higher up. But what were they so scared of?

Then he saw the dog. She must have crept through the grass on her tummy. Now she sped through the tussocks behind the fleeing hoppers.

She would never grab one before it escaped up here among the rocks. But the hoppers were so scared of the dog they hadn't noticed him — or his spear.

He readied himself as the first hopper bounded uphill.

His spear caught it in the belly. The hopper swivelled and fell in front of him, kicking with its long hind legs. The others bounded past him, terrified, while he quickly wrung the neck of the one at his feet. Its eyes glazed in death.

He kneeled and felt it. Thick, soft fur — he'd skin it and use it to keep off the rain and keep in the warmth — and good meat on those big legs. Even the tail looked fat.

The dog's wet nose nudged him.

'You want some of my hopper, girl?'

The dog glanced at him then back at the dead hopper.

And he understood what had just happened. The shock was so great he sat back, till the dog began to pull at the carcass.

'Not yet,' he said. He dug out his spear, then cut into the hopper and began to skin it, carefully tugging the hide from the meat. The dog patiently waited for her share of their hunt.

Our hunt, he thought. The dog had planned this. She had driven the hoppers to him, as he waited among the rocks above the grasslands.

Would she ever do it again?

He looked at her, panting in the sunlight. She almost seemed to be grinning.

He grinned too. Yes, he thought. We'll hunt that way again.

A man and dog were far more powerful than man or dog alone.

CHAPTER 47

# The Dog

The Rain Season

It rained, and then it rained again.

The world's scents changed. She lay on the highest rock to smell them, to learn what was out there: what food, what danger.

The land below their hill was sea and swamp now. The big hoppers had migrated to drier ground. Bony Boy could wade thigh-deep through the water, but the dog couldn't swim and hunt at the same time. The only food she could catch now lived on the rocky hills too: the small hoppers and lizards and birds she could creep up on.

Bony Boy still brought them fish every day, and sometimes a turtle too. He sat with them also, playing with the puppies, but not when it rained.

It rained so much now. Suddenly the air would thicken and the water washed down the ridges and across the rocks. Then, as suddenly as it had started, the rain would stop — until it rained again.

Bony Boy had brought them one of the huge, fat

swamp snakes this morning with enough meat for the whole pack. There was no need to hunt today.

She was bored. The puppies were bored too. As soon as the rain stopped they waddled out onto the rock, wrestling each other and sniffing in corners. She followed them, glad of the sunlight on her fur. The biggest of the puppies began to drag the snake skeleton out of the crevice, though he was too small to drag it far. One of the others waddled up and —

A shadow hovered above them. She had no time to growl, no time to leap.

Two massive bird legs lunged down. Talons snatched the biggest puppy. A few drops of blood splattered on the rock.

Then both bird and puppy were gone.

She grabbed a puppy by the scruff of its neck and hauled it into the crevice. The others followed, stumbling over each other in their eagerness to get into shelter. She left them huddled at the back of the crevice, then crept outside on her stomach, gazing up at the sky.

There was no sign of the bird.

The bird knew where they were now. Maybe it usually lived on the small hoppers. Now it could take all her puppies, picking them off one by one. She might be able to protect one or two, if they stayed close to her. But she couldn't protect them all.

She crawled back into the crevice. She grasped the smallest puppy by the scruff of its neck and dragged it out of the crevice, hoping the others had been frightened enough that they would stay hidden in their den and not try to follow her.

The rain fell again in fat drops. She ignored it as she trotted down the path.

CHAPTER 48

# Loa

It was a day to make you glad you had a deep overhang, a sloping floor to drain away any water that blew in, a fire and a roughly tanned hopper skin.

Mosquitoes hummed in a dark cloud above the swamp. Loa slapped more mud on his neck and legs to keep them off, then threw another branch on the fire. He watched it steam and began to shred more of the inner bark, tearing then twisting it into a growing length of string, then holding it over the flame to singe it just enough to be waterproof.

Some of the string would replace the fraying cord at his waist; he'd make a net from the rest. A fish net, a bird net, a bat net ... a net would have been useful when he and the dog had fought the monster lizard too.

He blinked as the dog appeared at the entrance of the overhang, her fur drenched, a wet puppy dangling from her mouth. It was the one he'd named Little Boy. She dropped the squirming puppy next to him, then turned around and vanished back into the rain.

What was she doing? Little Boy cowered, wet and trembling, on the muddy floor. Loa picked him up and put the puppy on his lap, tickling his tummy and scratching his ears till he stopped shivering, then offered him some of his cooked snake. The puppy's tiny teeth tore off a bit, just as the dog appeared again.

Another puppy!

Loa lifted the latest drenched puppy onto his lap too. He was glad the snake was a big one ...

It was only when the dog had brought the fourth puppy then settled herself between the fire and the ledge that he realised.

Four puppies. Not five. What had happened to the fifth?

This land had so many dangers for tiny puppies. She had brought them here for safety.

Little Girl wriggled off his lap. She padded over to the turtle shell where he kept fresh water. She lapped, then began to gnaw the edge of the shell.

Suddenly Loa felt like crying. It was like when his grandfather had given him his precious obsidian knife or when the younger boys of the clan had looked to him for guidance and help — the feeling of being connected and recognised.

The dog was saying, 'I trust you with my puppies.'

He looked over at her, her fur steaming in the fire's warmth. 'I'll look after you,' he said. 'I'll look after you all.'

CHAPTER 49

# The Dog

The scents this season were strong and rich, filled with life as well as the smells of water, mud and rotting wood.

It was time to teach the puppies about the world around them.

At first they tumbled after her as she climbed about the rocks and ledges between rainstorms, always in daylight, when Bony Boy was near.

As the season progressed and the rain eased to short showers each afternoon she took them out into the newly firm grasslands, green and rich from flood mud, the grasses long enough to hide them from birds of prey.

Several times she saw the grass shiver nearby as a croc moved stealthily towards them. Each time she ran. The puppies ran too.

The pups knew the scent of crocodile now; they knew the tracks it left in the mud, the swish it left with its tail.

She had them watch as she waited by the edge of the swamp, motionless, on her tummy, head down, till flocks of birds landed and began to feed, poking their beaks into the mud. In one sudden leap she grabbed one.

The smallest puppy learned fastest, but soon they could all manage it, even if they weren't successful every time.

They hunted frogs together, jumping frog-like themselves across the mud, crunching the frogs, bones and all. Fat mice scurried through the grass now too. The dogs crunched them in two gulps.

She showed the puppies how to mark their territory, squatting and letting out a few drops here, and then more there, so that any dog who passed would know who owned this land. She showed them how to sit on the highest rock and smell the world: scents of big hoppers returning to the grasslands; the small ones on the hills; and the scent of Bony Boy and his fire.

She taught them how to smell where Bony Boy had been and how to track the small hoppers too. They learned how to drive them towards Bony Boy and his spear and net, because that was the way to get most meat for dogs and human too.

Once she had hunted only before dawn and at dusk. But Bony Boy liked to hunt in early and late daylight. Somehow she had become a dog of the daylight too, waiting for him to feed her and the puppies with hunks of hopper or pulling out the innards in a big steaming heap for them to nose through.

The two smallest puppies were even more daylight dogs than she was. Bony Boy was their family: they slept curled up with him and played with him during the day, tugging on sticks he held or leaping up for bits of meat or bones. They were almost full-grown now, but they still clambered onto his lap, till he laughed and complained about their weight and the smell of wet fur. He stroked their heads or scratched their backs or rubbed off leeches in a way that meant the bites didn't itch.

The bigger two slept further and further from the fire now they were large enough not to need Bony Boy's protection. Sometimes they slunk off by themselves, coming back with feathers around their mouths, sleeping when she and Little Boy and Little Girl followed Bony Boy down the track to hunt.

She watched and understood.

Then one dawn she took them through the mangroves. They hunted frogs, snapping and jumping, more for fun than hunger. She sniffed the air. There was a danger scent. Where was it? She lifted her nose again.

Suddenly the bigger two pups broke away. They padded through the mud and shadows to where the water still ran in a shallow river at the edge of the swamp. She watched as they paddled into the river then began to swim away from them. She knew at once what they were doing. They were finding their own territory across the river.

The ripples changed upstream. A log became a crocodile. It had been a croc all the time they'd been here. It must have swum close last night while they slept.

'Yip!' she yelped, desperately hoping they would hear and understand. She ran to the edge of the river and yelped again, trying to make the croc head for her instead.

It didn't. The croc knew her pups were easier meat. She watched it, a silent shape sliding through the water. Could she swim to it to distract it? She leaped into the water — then stopped.

The young dogs were on the other side now. They didn't wait to shake themselves dry. They had seen the croc too, or felt its movement in the water. She yipped another warning. They ran, swift and steady through the mangroves, till they were two shadows lost among the others.

She waded back to dry land. She could smell their scent getting fainter and fainter, as they ran beyond their mother's territory to find their own. She could smell their paw prints as she padded back through the mangroves, the other two young dogs at her side. They headed up the track to Bony Boy. He was the centre of her pack now. Her home.

That night she left the two young dogs curled up with Bony Boy. She climbed to the highest hill, as the moon cast its shadows on the world. She lifted up her head and sang.

It was a song of love, of loss, of understanding. It said, 'I am here; and you are there.'

At last she stopped, and listened. For the first time in this new land she heard the howl back.

Her children were there. Not here, but safe.

This was a land of dogs now.

She howled once more and heard them answer again.

Then she padded back down the hill to Bony Boy and his dogs.

CHAPTER 50

# Loa

## The Season of Fruit and Flowers

Loa gazed out across his land as the first of the sunlight glinted on the rocks. Little Boy and Little Girl sat next to him, chewing hopper bones from yesterday's hunt. He only had to say 'down' now and they'd sit and then roll over, waiting for their treat. Beside them the fire flickered and flared.

The river had shrunk to a clear sweep of water down one end of the swamp; the once-submerged grasslands were again hard and flat and just beginning to brown off. Flocks of birds bobbed among the grass seeds.

The dog was out there, somewhere. Even as he thought it he heard her howl from the top of the ridge.

'Hrrrrrl! Hrrrllll!'

The sound echoed across the rocks and another call came from the far-off hill towards the sea.

'Hrrrl! Hrrrl!'

Little Boy and Little Girl stopped chewing to listen, but they didn't answer back.

So Big Boy and Big Girl were safe. He'd worried when they hadn't come back one day with the other dogs. He grinned. Three dogs were enough for any hunter.

'Hrrrl!' That was the dog's call again. Loa leaned back against the rock. He and the dogs would hunt again this morning, before the hoppers went to the shade of their midday resting places. Little Boy and Little Girl were getting even better at herding the game his way. Sometimes the three dogs even brought the game down themselves. But these days the dog knew to let him take the skin, the bladder and whatever else he wanted before they dragged away the rest. He smiled. Little Boy and Little Girl obeyed him every time he gave an order. Their mother obeyed only when she wanted to.

He had more spears now, with good bone points. He still used his obsidian knife as a spearhead for hunting hoppers and large birds, but the bone-headed spears were good enough to fish with.

Maybe we won't hunt hoppers today, he thought, idly rubbing Little Girl's ears. He never tried to rub the dog's ears — she might nip his hand. He could fish from the river bank — his fish hooks were useful now, strong enough to catch the biggest fish. This was the season for turtle and crocodile eggs. The dogs sniffed out the nests easily, crunching the soft bones of the baby crocs and turtles in the eggs. There were a couple of crocs near now, a big one and a small one towards the sea. He watched for their tracks every day, making sure he knew exactly where they were. The dogs seemed to be able to sniff out crocs as well as their nests too. They were so big now that no other animal could catch them.

Suddenly he sat straighter, staring at the horizon. Smoke!

Another wildfire? But this grass was still too green to burn easily. He hadn't heard thunder either. This smoke hung like a necklace in the sky: it was a campfire.

People.

For a moment all he felt was joy. He hadn't allowed himself to feel lonely this past season, but now it came swelling back like a storm tide.

Men to hunt with. Women's laughter, songs and stories around the fire. He had dreamed of finding people for so long. Reality struck him like a wave in the face. These people would be strangers — as strange, perhaps, as this new land he was just coming to know. He'd had no idea back when he'd landed just how different this country and its animals were from all he'd known. Worse — to the people here he would be a stranger too. And, he remembered, his dogs might be strangest of all. There were no other packs here.

A stranger might be an enemy. The unknown was always frightening.

Back home clans spoke different languages. The further away they were the more their language was different. He could learn a new language — but not in time to say, 'I want to be a friend. I am a stranger in a new land. I will take to your ways. Just let me live.'

What if these people were head-hunters? The grandfathers told stories of clans who killed strangers and hung their skulls on trees around their camps.

He swallowed. What if the people who lived here were really different, just like the hoppers weren't like any animal he'd ever seen? Maybe they had tails, or swung from trees. Maybe this really was the land of ghosts ...

Stop it, he told himself. You're a man, not a boy to be frightened by stories around a campfire. But a wise man, a hunter, should be cautious.

He held himself straighter. He *was* a hunter. He could move silently, a shadow among the trees, so no one could see him. The dogs moved silently too. Rubbish dogs were good at silence, at slinking around the edges of a camp. The dogs would scent out people long before they might see him.

He'd find these people and watch them, silently, secretly; he'd make sure of them before they even knew he was there.

He had learned to live with this new land. Now it was time to learn its people too.

CHAPTER 51

# Loa

He cut that afternoon's fish into long thin strips, enough for him and the dogs to eat for the next couple of days, then hung it over a green wood fire overnight. The smoke and dryness would stop the strips spoiling.

He covered his campfire with dry bones, and then big logs, damp from the swamp. The coals should stay slowly burning for days, but with almost no smoke — he didn't want the strangers to see it till he knew more about them.

The strangers' smoke still lazily spiralled into the sky. He headed towards it, the dogs padding at his heels.

The dogs stayed with him all day, skirting around rainwater lakes covered in water lilies, keeping to the high ground where the grass was shorter and the going easier. Clouds of birds flapped into the sky as they passed. I'll need to be careful, he thought. The birds' alarm might give him away.

He climbed up onto a hill, away from crocodiles. The strangers' campfire smoke was close now, possibly only a few bends along the river that curled below them. But no one would find him here. People stayed by their campfires at night, unless they were ghosts, nightwalkers roaming the shadows ...

No ghosts! he told himself firmly. And if they were ... he could make a raft and paddle along the coast where the ghosts wouldn't find him. But would the dogs follow him onto a raft? What if they jumped off and tried to swim to shore?

Little Boy and Little Girl might let him tie them up. But the dog was too wise to be tricked. Nor did he want to do it: you didn't trick your friends.

All at once he knew how much the dogs meant to him. They were his family, his clan, his hunting partners. Had anyone ever had a friendship with animals like this before?

He didn't know. But he couldn't part with the dogs now.

The dog stood up in what could have been a signal. Little Girl and Little Boy stood up too. The dogs vanished into the shadows, returning almost immediately with a long-necked bird each. The younger dogs dropped their birds at Loa's feet. They sat obediently while he plucked them. He waited till they'd rolled over, then let them sit up and gave them back their birds, eating the smoked fish himself.

Darkness gathered like a woven basket across the sky. The moon rose, soft looking and silky. The darkness turned to shadows in the moonlight.

He stood and signalled the dogs to be quiet. It was silly to sign to dogs, he knew — they didn't know the hunting signals. And they always were quiet! But it felt right.

He trod carefully down the hill, then walked along the river, trusting the dogs to scent crocodile or snake. He could smell campfire smoke now and the fatty scent of charred hopper. The dogs lifted their noses. He was glad they'd just eaten. He thought they'd be wary of strange humans, just as he was, but at least they wouldn't be tempted too close by hunger.

He looked at them, his shadow companions, almost the same colour as the moonlit grass. What if the strangers speared his dogs?

Suddenly he was more scared for them than himself. The dog knew that humans could be dangerous. But Little Boy and Little Girl had known only him. He imagined Little Girl bleeding in the grass; or Little Boy with a spear through his side. He could hardly explain the dogs were his friends if he didn't know the strangers' language.

All at once he wanted to gather the dogs to him, to carry them away where they'd be safe. If only he hadn't brought them with him! Though in fact the dogs had brought themselves. Dogs went where they wanted to, even if they came when you called them — most of the time. He had no way to make them stay.

Please, he thought, stay with me now. Don't go near the strangers, no matter how interesting they smell. Stay.

Flames rippled around the next bend, the fire reflected in the water. Another few steps and he could see the fire itself, and then the figures around it.

'Sit,' he whispered, soft as a breath of wind. Little Boy and Little Girl sat. The dog looked at Loa, then at her puppies. She didn't sit. But she didn't leave his side either.

He let out a breath he hadn't known he'd been holding, then looked at the strangers more closely.

They were as human as himself. Not ghosts. No tails either. A few wore strange breechcloths or necklaces, but others were naked.

They could almost have been his own clan, only taller and more long-legged, though maybe that was the effect of the leaping shadows from the flames. A few grandfathers and grandmothers, younger women with babies, children already curling up to sleep near the fire. A couple of men rubbed fat into their spears. They were longer and thicker than his weapons, he thought.

Something cold nudged his leg. It was Little Girl, trying to get his attention. She looked at him and then at the camp, as though to say, 'Are we going there?'

The dog looked at him too. She seemed as wary of the strangers as he was. Did she remember being tied up by the cooking pit? He shook his head at Little Girl, though he didn't think she understood the gesture. But they understood when he began to creep away. They stayed at his side, as quiet as the moon.

CHAPTER 52

# Loa

He had only meant to doze then leave in the pre-dawn light. But yesterday's walk — and the relief of finding humans — had tired him more than he'd thought.

The sunlight on his face woke him. He sat up suddenly and looked around, alarmed.

Where were the younger dogs? Had they wandered near the camp? Maybe they were already dog meat ...

He scrambled to his feet, then saw them sitting on the rock, comfortably surveying the world below. If they'd hunted earlier there was no sign of it. And if they had, he realised with relief, no one had seen them.

He heard voices in the distance, further away than last night's camp.

Good, he thought. No one was coming this way.

He needed time — time to get back to his own camp, time to think about how he could make the strangers see the dogs as friends, not food, to show them how good a partnership between dogs and humans could be. To see him not as some magician who could talk to animals, or even as an enemy who'd come sneaking by to steal a woman, but as exactly what he was —

a young man who had lost his own people and was prepared to take on another clan's language and ways.

As long as they spared his dogs.

He strode down the hill, keeping away from the river, where men might be silently fishing or women catching birds. He didn't stop to drink. The dogs did — there was no way he could stop them and he couldn't risk calling them. But finally the river was behind them. The world was silent, dawn's bird chorus done for the day. Only one more lake through the grasslands ...

The birds that had flown away the day before weren't there today. Maybe a crocodile had scared them —

He saw her then. But realised she'd seen him first. She stood immobile: she was long-limbed, her skin as dark as the water, her eyes wide and scared. She was a little younger than he was, perhaps. He saw when she saw the dogs too, her eyes widening as she wondered whether to run from the strange man and the strange beasts, or if running would just make them chase her.

'Sit,' he whispered to the dogs. Little Boy and Little Girl sat obediently. The dog glanced at her puppies, then at Loa, then at the girl. Finally she decided to sit too, scratching her ear with her hind leg.

The girl stared at Loa and at the dogs. She looked scared, but curious too.

Loa tried a smile. 'Hello.'

The girl said something he didn't understand.

Loa put his spear down, then lifted his hands to show he held no weapons. He reached down and scratched Little Boy behind the ears. The dog grinned. Little Girl rolled over to let him scratch her tummy.

The dog gazed at the girl. The girl gazed back, then at Loa, fascination battling with fear.

How could he say, 'Don't be scared of us'? How could he show her he wasn't going to try to capture her, or hurt her, and that the dogs wouldn't hurt her either?

Suddenly Little Girl stood up. Before he could stop her she padded over to the girl. She sniffed the girl's legs, curiously, then snuffled at a woven bag lying in the grass. She sat at the girl's feet, looking up hopefully. Loa wondered if the bag held mussels or maybe wood grubs. He didn't know how to ask.

The girl looked at Loa, looked at Little Boy and the dog, then at Little Girl, still sitting at her feet, mouth open in a doggy grin. Slowly, very slowly, the girl reached out and touched Little Girl's head, then darted her fingers away, as though she was scared she'd be bitten.

'Grrf,' said Little Girl, drooling at the scent of whatever was in the basket.

Loa reached down and scratched Little Boy's ears again. The girl gave a delighted giggle as she bent down and scratched Little Girl the same way. The young dog shut her eyes in pleasure.

The girl looked at Loa, a true smile on her face now as she scratched Little Girl just the way he was scratching Little Boy. He smiled back at her, admiring her courage. She must have seen Little Girl's sharp teeth. Any of the girls back home would have run away screaming. But this girl touched a strong and frightening animal. This girl smiled at a stranger.

The dog gazed at them, wary.

He wanted to stay with the girl. Learn how to talk to her, ask her to take him to her family. But he had to think about the dogs too.

Suddenly Loa knew what to do.

He held up his hand and pointed towards his far-off camp. He gestured at himself, then at the dogs, then at the camp again. Then he pointed towards the girl's camp, made a beckoning gesture, then pointed to his camp again. The signals were the only way he knew how to say, 'I'm taking the dogs back to my camp. Tell your people to come to my camp too.'

The girl stared at him. Did she understand?

Someone called from back towards the river. The girl called something in return.

He had to go. Now. Fast, before a hunter could find them and cast a spear: at the dogs for food; at him in case he was attacking or stealing the girl. He had to hope she'd tell them he wasn't an enemy, that his dogs were strange, but not dangerous or for eating.

He smiled at her one last time. She smiled back, her face like the sun edging above the mountains, like the moon lifting out of the seas.

He began to jog into the grasslands. The dogs pranced after him.

He glanced back. The girl watched him. He wondered what she saw, then looked at her face and knew.

She saw a hunter. A man, his muscles stronger from the last hard year of work, not the boy he'd been such a short time earlier. A man who could survive alone, who could make a camp from nothing. A warrior who commanded animals.

That's me, he thought. That's who I am now.

The voices were closer now. He began to run through the grass, the dogs trotting on either side. But his mind's eye still saw the girl.

CHAPTER 53

# Loa

Dusk crept across the world as he drew near to his own camp. The coals of his fire were still glowing. He threw more wood on, knowing it was too dark for the strangers to see his smoke tonight. He wanted the girl's clan to find him, but not for a few days yet.

He speared a fish at first light, taking the time to feed it bit at a time to the dogs, making sure that Little Girl and Little Boy sat and rolled over obediently every time he gave the word.

The dog looked bored, as though it was her right to share the fish without all the sitting and rolling. He agreed with her, but worry tugged at him. If only there was some way to tell her that she would be safer if she was tamer.

But he knew her as well as she knew him. She did what she wanted.

He headed back to his camp and began to dig a pit, glad the soil wasn't yet the hard almost-rock of the Dry. It was hard work, loosening the soil with a stick, scraping it out with a giant bailer shell carried here by a tide at the height of the Rain.

It took a day to make the pit big enough. He ate turtle eggs because he didn't want to spare time to hunt, but he still made sure that Little Girl and Little Boy sat and rolled over each time before they ate. He gathered rocks, flinging them into the pit, then firewood, as dry as he could find.

At night he dreamed of the girl.

Now it was time to hunt.

'Dog!'

He never knew if she'd come when he called or not. But today her golden shape appeared on the path, the younger dogs behind her.

He lifted his hunting spear. 'Hunt,' he said. 'Hunt, girl.'

He didn't know if the dog understood his words. But she knew what it meant when he lifted his spear and gazed at the hoppers then at her.

She gave a doggy grin, her tongue lolling, then slunk off into the still-long grass. The younger dogs followed her.

Loa waited for them to drive the hoppers towards him, his spear in his hands.

CHAPTER 54

# Loa

The dogs howled that night, the first time since he'd seen the strangers' campfire smoke. It was almost as though they knew that it was time to call them.

The girl's father, brothers, uncles and grandfathers would never have heard a dog's howl before: they'd come to investigate.

He hoped they'd come as friends, not enemies. Had the girl explained? Had she understood?

He thought of her smile, the way she'd giggled when she touched Little Girl. If anyone could understand it would be her.

He put green wood on the fire the next morning, to make the most smoke to show the girl's clan exactly where his camp was. They'd know that much smoke must be a signal, a way of saying, 'Here I am.' It could be an invitation — or a threat. In the fire pit the two hoppers lay cooking, hot and moist and tasty under the layer of wet leaves and soil, away from flies. Food in a fire pit kept good for days.

He put on his necklaces of fish vertebrae and hopper teeth. He sat on the ledge by his campfire and rubbed hopper fat into his spears so they gleamed, their shafts thick and straight; they were obviously made by a hunter who knew what he was doing. His obsidian knife hung by the cord about his waist. Little Boy and Little Girl slept beside him. The dog was off somewhere, hunting perhaps, tired of eating eggs.

Suddenly the young dogs' ears pricked. Little Girl sat up, glancing across at Loa as though to say, 'Can't you hear them too?'

At first all he could see was grass moving, as though a giant snake was coming towards them. The ripple grew nearer. It was made by people.

The whole clan had come, not just the hunters, men who might attack a stranger. The girl had convinced her clan that he wasn't luring them to battle. They had understood each other well that day. He could see a couple of grandmothers, some grandfathers, white hair and long white beards, women with babies slung on their backs, keeping their hands free to carry bags filled with fruits and tubers they had gathered on the way.

Two of the hunters had long-necked birds slung over their shoulders. Loa would have grinned if he hadn't been so nervous. The hunters didn't know a feast waited for them.

The girl walked behind the others. He'd hoped she'd be in the front, as eager to see him again as he was to see her, but of course the hunters would lead the clan. Then he saw that she too wore necklaces — shells and bright red seeds.

She wore them for him.

He stood up so she could see him, so they could all see him. He wanted to smile at the girl, but her uncles might resent a stranger smiling so openly before he'd proved his worth. Little Girl and Little Boy stood too, yawning.

Suddenly one of the hunters raised his spear. He aimed at Little Girl ...

'Down!' But even as Loa gave the order the girl ran forwards and grabbed the man's spear arm. She spoke to him urgently. The hunter lowered his spear. The man stared as Little Girl and Little Boy sat at Loa's feet, just as he'd planned, then rolled onto their backs.

But where is the dog? thought Loa frantically. He needed her to be here too, so everyone would see he had three tame dogs, not just two. He bent slowly, and scratched the dogs' tummies, listening to the mutters of wonder from the strangers.

All at once a grandma pointed.

The dog stood on the rock above them. It's almost as though she's inviting a spear, thought Loa desperately.

'Dog!' he called, hoping she'd come. Hoping they'd realise that if she did come running down it was because he'd ordered her to, not because she was attacking. He remembered how he'd thrown stones at the rubbish dogs, before he'd known that a human and an animal could be friends and partners.

The dog vanished off the rock. Suddenly she appeared on the path, running towards them, a bird dangling from her mouth.

The hunter raised his spear again. Loa could almost hear the man think, I'll be the first to kill the new beast. The girl said something, quickly and firmly. But the hunter shrugged her off. This was men's business.

The spear was long and well made, its point sharp. At this range the hunter wouldn't miss.

'Dog!' he cried desperately.

The dog glanced at him as she ran down the path towards him. There was something in her look that said she knew exactly what was happening, and what she was doing now.

She looked almost amused as she ran up to Loa. She dropped the bird at his feet and glanced up at him again, as if to say, 'I'm doing this for you.' Then rolled over, her legs in the air.

It was as though she shouted to every human here: 'Look! This man is my master! I catch food for him. We dogs are useful. Let us live.'

The hunter put down his spear. Someone laughed. All at once they were all laughing — the grandmothers, the hunters, the girl, even the toddlers on the women's backs. They pointed at the dogs and at Loa.

Loa laughed too. He bent down to scratch the dogs' tummies so the strangers wouldn't see his tears.

A shadow crossed his. It was the girl. She bent down beside him, then, cautiously at first, began to scratch Little Girl's tummy too.

Soon, he thought, when I can breathe again, I'll show them all the fire pit and the feast I prepared. Show the girl's uncles that he was a hunter to be respected and a spear maker, as well as the man who'd tamed the dogs. He'd show the girl too.

He smiled, and met her eyes.

'Arrunna,' she said.

He didn't know if that was her name, or 'hello' in her language, or maybe a word for 'strange animal that likes to be scratched'.

It didn't matter. They understood each other in all the ways that mattered now. There would be long happy years to find out more. Somehow he knew that from now on things would be good, for him and for the dogs too. His dogs. His friends.

'Loa,' he said, and reached over to scratch the dog, his hand next to the girl's.

EPILOGUE

# The Dog

## The Thunder Season

It was hot. The ground breathed dryness into the air. Soon the winds would bring the rains again, but today the soil was too warm under her paws.

The dog was tired. Today's hunt had been short. Many dogs had flushed out the mob of big hoppers for the men to spear. Two of the men carried the great beasts back to the camp.

But she was old. Too weary to walk any more just now. She lay on the grass, panting, then put her head on her paws.

Bony Boy looked down at her. He was tall and muscular, not bony at all, but the dog still thought of him as she had when they first met. 'You tired, old dog?'

The dog whined softly.

Bony Boy grinned. He kneeled in the grass and lifted her expertly, so she lay across his shoulders, front and back paws dangling each side of his neck. He strode through the grass after the other hunters, bearing her on his shoulders, his big hands gently holding her paws.

There was no need to walk when she was tired now, not with Bony Boy to carry her.

Tonight there'd be a feast around the fire. There'd be bones to chew, for her and the other dogs, her puppies and her children's children too. But Bony Boy would make sure she had the best bits of all, the squishy parts she loved most. Perhaps tonight she'd hear howls from the darkness, where her wild children and their pups hunted for themselves.

The dog let herself enjoy the rocking motion as Bony Boy walked, the smell of fresh meat, the warmth of the sun.

It was a good day to be a dingo.

# AUTHOR'S NOTES

Probably the first explanation I need to give here is that dingoes don't bark — and nor would their ancestors have barked either. This is why none of the dogs bark in this book.

This is not a true story, but it is what might have happened.

This is a story from five to ten thousand years ago, but probably closer to five, as testing of wild dingoes' DNA and RNA tells us that was likely when the first dingo arrived in Australia, probably from Timor or one of the islands nearby. (If dingoes had arrived much before ten thousand years ago they would have reached Tasmania, as Tasmania was still connected to the mainland then.)

The earliest dingo skeleton found so far is about three and a half thousand years old, but it's likely there were dingoes in Australia long before that.

Dingoes are so similar genetically that it is likely that all the modern packs are descended from one pregnant female. How did she come to be here, one dog, so long ago?

Some stories teach us our history. Others tell us what it might have been like. They're a window on the past and say, 'This is what could have happened.'

This story is one of those.

There are many other versions of how the dingo first arrived in Australia. Many of them belong to the Indigenous people of the north and all of them differ.

We know little about that time. What we do know is derived from ancient tools, the remnants of plants, middens with shells and pieces of bone and stone-lined ovens, as well as from old histories passed down through many generations. Ancient adzes tell us that Loa's people would have had the tools to make canoes; and the lack of shards of pottery means that they probably didn't know how to make pots.

We also know that at that time, at the end of the last Ice Age, the sea level was about one hundred metres lower than it is now — much of the world's water was still locked up as ice. The camp that Loa came from, and the coast where he arrived, would be underwater now, and probably very different from the land as it is now, although the seasons and many of the plants would be similar.

Even if the sea level had been higher when the first dingoes arrived, earlier than we now think, the first dog must have come here across at least fifty-five kilometres of sea, too far for a dog to swim. Possibly, as in this book, the first dog arrived in a canoe lost in a storm. Later, thousands of years later, when sails and better canoes and then other craft had been invented, traders would regularly cross those waters, as well as fishermen. But not back then.

**Blood and guts**

Apologies, but this is a book about a dog, and set five thousand years ago. Meat and hunting was what kept life going then. They still do for a wild dog. We can pretend that what comes in a can or as dried dog food wasn't once alive, but what you buy in a can probably came from an animal that suffered more before its death than the swift kills made by Loa and the dogs in this book.

I wanted to write a book about the discovery of humanity's closest friendship — the one we enjoy with domesticated dogs. But to do it I needed to write about things most of us would rather not think of.

**The dog as food**

Even in the last few hundred years, Macassan and Torres Strait fishermen would take a dog out in their boats as a way of storing food, or to throw to a shark or crocodile if a diver was threatened. I know it will be confronting to many who love dogs to know that dogs were — and still in many places are — valued more as dinner than as friends. But that too is the way things are and have been.

**The seasons**

Loa's people would have measured time by at least four seasons, possibly five or six or more. I have limited them to four in this book.

*The Dry Season — May to late September/early October*

It does rain at this time, but the air is dry, not humid.

The early Dry Season can be a season all to itself, with fat tubers and lots of fruit. Later the grass turns gold, then vanishes from the soil. In July and August there are less fruit and fewer tubers to dig and animals to hunt. What was once swamp dries out and cracks.

*The Thunder Season — October and November*
In this season there is thunder in the air and occasional storms. The grass grows green and tall, and massive tides bring new water to the mangrove swamps.

*The Rain/Wet Season — December to early March*
This is the season when monsoons, cyclones and big storms may blow in from the sea, when swamps turn to rivers and grasslands turn to swamps.

*The Season of Fruit and Flowers — March and April*
The season of grass seeds and fruit, bringing flocks of birds.

**Dingoes**
Dingoes are close to the original wolves that first formed a partnership with humans. Most other dog breeds have been deliberately bred to be small, or lovable, or fetch sticks or game. Dingoes are about as close as we have now to the original wild dog ancestor.

Dogs were first domesticated in the Middle East and the Americas, and travelled from there to South-East Asia. Australian dingoes have Chinese or South-

East Asian ancestors, although they are quite different from modern South-East Asian dogs.

But today's dingoes are probably not quite like the ones who arrived here, who were even closer to being wild dogs, living on the edge of human camps scavenging for food, and often becoming food themselves. (It's worth remembering that dogs thought of humans as food too, as did many other animals nearby.)

Dingoes don't bark as domesticated dogs do. They breed only once a year — dogs breed twice. Only the dominant female dingo in a pack breeds, with the dominant male. The dominant female feeds first too, and then the others. All the others are uncles or aunts who help bring up the puppies. The pack also hunts together, although dingoes will hunt by themselves often too. Nearly all domestic dogs can breed with them — and will unless they are kept apart or desexed, which is one reason why dingoes are becoming an endangered species. Many of the animals we think of as 'dingoes' are actually part dog.

Dingoes are far more independent than most dogs. They'll go along with what a human wants ... most of the time. But they may think about it first.

A dingo hunts quietly and swiftly, often waiting lying on its tummy for prey to arrive rather than chasing it wildly, then leaping at the throat. Dingoes are very efficient hunters and soon became a problem when white settlers brought sheep to the continent. Dingoes were used to hunting wary prey. Sheep, especially before they have been shorn and are carrying heavy woollen fleeces, are slow and nervous and most breeds aren't very bright, making them remarkably easy for dingoes to hunt and kill.

But even though they are efficient hunters, dingoes aren't aggressive. They can and do fight and bite, but usually only when they — or more usually their puppies — are threatened.

Dingoes changed Australia, possibly helping to wipe out many species like the thylacine and Tasmanian devil on the mainland and helping humans to hunt, as well as providing companionship and joy. Australia also changed the first dogs here, as they became dingoes.

Domesticated dogs arrived with the First Fleet. They were largely accepted by many Indigenous people as, unlike dingoes, the 'new' dogs would bark to warn of intruders. Dogs — and dingoes — were soon adopted by the people of Tasmania, who until then had never worked with canines.

Governor Arthur Phillip and Captain Hunter also adopted dingoes as pets, but more often the new settlers shot, trapped or poisoned them. The last wild dingoes in my area of New South Wales were killed in the early 1970s, courtesy of a government scheme that dropped poisoned baits to wipe them out. Most dingo traps were cruel — a dingo might even gnaw its own leg off to try to get free — leaving animals in pain to die slowly of thirst or blood loss.

Now, after so long, dingoes may become a tamed species, not just because so many are killed in places where they can become a nuisance for people, but because they are breeding with feral dogs.

Nowadays there are breeding programmes that try to bolster numbers of 'pure' dingoes, both the gold and the black ones, using DNA tests to make sure they are dingoes, not a dog–dingo hybrid that just looks right.

Most 'wild dingoes' probably do have some dog in their ancestry — and the proportion is growing. The last large area of 'pure' wild dingoes was Kakadu National Park, but now even many of the dingoes tested there are hybrids. Fraser Island once had a large colony of pure dingoes, but the most recent study there showed that about a third were hybrids — and those hybrids will probably breed with the others.

It is legal in some states to have a dingo as a pet, but this is carefully regulated. I won't give details here, as the regulations often change. Dingoes are loyal companions — once a dingo has bonded with you it may not ever regard anyone else as its partner. But never think a dingo is an easy pet. A companion dingo is beautiful, strong, wise, funny and determined. But every dingo is still, despite so many generations of association with humans, very much its own creature. Never approach a wild dingo, or try to tame one as Loa did. Dingoes may attack if stirred or threatened — but they can also see you as a threat, even if you don't mean to be.

**Dingo life cycle**

Australian dingo puppies are generally born after a sixty-three-day gestation between March and June. There are usually about four to six in a litter. At first the puppies' eyes are closed and they drink only milk.

Later they eat meat that the mother has chewed and partly digested and vomited up for them; and after that they begin to eat the food she — or the rest of the pack — bring back for them. Slowly they learn to hunt and track, following the others as they learn their skills.

Dingo pups are weaned at about two months of age and within a year most are independent, some staying with the pack but more moving on to make a new pack, or joining another. Male dingoes can breed once they are about a year old. So can female dingoes, but often they don't until they are two years old.

Young dingoes can have their first puppies slightly out of the normal season, as the one in this book did.

**The name 'dingo'**

The Eora people who lived around Sydney Harbour called wild dogs 'warrigal'. Tame dogs were known as 'tingo', and that is where we got the name 'dingo'. Loa's language would have been very different from any language spoken today, just as the English we speak today is utterly changed from the English spoken a thousand years ago. I haven't tried to recreate that language, and so have used the modern word 'dingo'. Loa uses the word 'dog' — the word he'd have used in his own language for the animals he knew.

**Why are there no coconuts, sails or wild millet in this story?**

This story is set at least five thousand years ago. Coconuts probably hadn't been brought to the islands north of Australia at that stage — and certainly not to the mainland. Millet doesn't seem to have been gathered yet and sails still weren't used in this part of the world.

The coastline was very different too. It's likely that the land Loa set out from, and the place he landed, are underwater today. The swamps and to some extent even the river systems would have been different too. None of the places in this book are based on any specific area that exists now.

**Loa's knee**

Loa didn't break his leg when the canoe crashed. Instead he tore his medial collateral ligament — the same injury I had while I wrote the book. The medial ligament holds the kneecap in place. It can be agonisingly painful, as when the kneecap moves it tears more flesh and ligaments, but if you keep the knee immobilised — and you're lucky — it does heal. (I tore my knee climbing down a cliff without a rope to look at what I thought might be a rare plant. It wasn't — and I was silly and careless. And many thanks indeed to Nicol for helping my knee heal much faster and less painfully than Loa's.)

With all the benefits of modern health care, I knew my knee would eventually heal. Loa would have feared that he'd be a cripple forever.

**The dog's name**

Most of us give human names to the animals we are close to, but this wasn't always so. It would probably never have occurred to Loa to name the dog. It may have taken many generations of dogs and humans living together for humans to realise that a dog could learn a particular name, and come or obey when that word was used.

Many humans who are close to an animal still don't give their animal friends a human name. I've known farmers and bushies who just call their companion 'Dog' or 'Hey You'. I call one of the wombats who shares my life 'Wombat', although to others she is known as 'Mothball'.

Names are human devices, not animal. Animals just learn — sometimes — what we mean when we use them. But sharing your life with an animal — whether it is a dog, cat, horse or wombat — is one of the greatest joys and privileges a human can have.

# ACKNOWLEDGEMENTS

It is difficult to know where to start with thanks for a book like this. Its existence is owed to the many researchers in ethnobotany, anthropology, zoology and many other disciplines that enabled me to recreate the world of so long ago, as well as the dedication and empathy of the many people who have worked with and studied dingoes. Thanks are due not just for the research this book is based on, but for opening the ever-fascinating complexities of the world to others.

As always, enormous thanks to Lisa Berryman, for giving me the freedom to follow my inspiration, even when it isn't for the book that was on the schedule, and for her ever-wonderful assessments, encouragement and insistence that each manuscript reach its highest possible potential.

Kate Burnitt has worked and reworked this book, picking up errors and inconsistencies. If Loa no longer gets into a canoe twice without getting out of it — and many similar mistakes — it is entirely due to Kate, with her endless perfectionism and patience.

Angela Marshall as always performed the miracle of turning what many might find gibberish into a properly spelled manuscript, as well as giving her own extraordinary depth of knowledge both to Loa's world and the intimacies of canine behaviour. Again — and again — much love and so many, many thanks. I hope that your students will find that this book speaks to them too.

To my husband Bryan, who probably will read neither these acknowledgements nor the book (he prefers books with diagrams, and preferably submarines), my love and gratitude always, for letting me expound my theories of the ancient world while you pretend to listen, your eyes almost imperceptibly flicking over your *New Scientist* or computer screen.

And finally — this book, and at least two others, wouldn't have been written without the loving inspiration of Hank Huffington, to whom this book is dedicated.

# *Titles by Jackie French*

## *Australian Historical*

*Somewhere Around the Corner • Dancing with Ben Hall*
*Daughter of the Regiment • Soldier on the Hill*
*Tom Appleby, Convict Boy • A Rose for the Anzac Boys*
*The Night They Stormed Eureka • Nanberry: Black Brother White*
*Pennies for Hitler*

## *General Historical*

*Hitler's Daughter • Lady Dance • How the Finnegans Saved the Ship*
*The White Ship • Valley of Gold • They Came on Viking Ships*
*Macbeth and Son • Pharaoh • Oracle • I am Juliet*
*Ophelia: Queen of Denmark*

## *Fiction*

*Rain Stones • Walking the Boundaries • The Secret Beach*
*Summerland • A Wombat Named Bosco • Beyond the Boundaries*
*The Warrior: The Story of a Wombat*
*The Book of Unicorns • Tajore Arkle*
*Missing You, Love Sara • Dark Wind Blowing*
*Ride the Wild Wind: The Golden Pony and Other Stories*
*Refuge • The Book of Horses and Unicorns*

## *Non-Fiction*

*Seasons of Content • How the Aliens from Alpha Centauri*
*Invaded My Maths Class and Turned Me into a Writer*
*How to Guzzle Your Garden • The Book of Challenges*
*Stamp, Stomp, Whomp • The Fascinating History of Your Lunch*
*Big Burps, Bare Bums and Other Bad-Mannered Blunders*
*To the Moon and Back • Rocket Your Child into Reading*
*The Secret World of Wombats*
*How High Can a Kangaroo Hop? • A Year in the Valley*
*Let the Land Speak: How the Land Created Our Nation*
*I Spy a Great Reader*

## *The Animal Stars Series*

*The Goat Who Sailed the World • The Dog Who Loved a Queen*
*The Camel Who Crossed Australia*
*The Donkey Who Carried the Wounded*
*The Horse Who Bit a Bushranger*
*Dingo: The Dog Who Conquered a Continent*

## *The Matilda Saga*

*1. A Waltz for Matilda • 2. The Girl from Snowy River*
*3. The Road to Gundagai • 4. To Love a Sunburnt Country*
*5. The Ghost by the Billabong*

## *The Secret Histories Series*

*Birrung the Secret Friend • Barney and the Secret of the Whales*

## *Outlands Trilogy*

*In the Blood • Blood Moon • Flesh and Blood*

## *School for Heroes Series*

*Lessons for a Werewolf Warrior • Dance of the Deadly Dinosaurs*

## *Wacky Families Series*

*1. My Dog the Dinosaur • 2. My Mum the Pirate*
*3. My Dad the Dragon • 4. My Uncle Gus the Garden Gnome*
*5. My Uncle Wal the Werewolf • 6. My Gran the Gorilla*
*7. My Auntie Chook the Vampire Chicken • 8. My Pa the Polar Bear*

## *Phredde Series*

*1. A Phaery Named Phredde*
*2. Phredde and a Frog Named Bruce*
*3. Phredde and the Zombie Librarian*
*4. Phredde and the Temple of Gloom*
*5. Phredde and the Leopard-Skin Librarian*
*6. Phredde and the Purple Pyramid*
*7. Phredde and the Vampire Footy Team*
*8. Phredde and the Ghostly Underpants*

## *Picture Books*

*Diary of a Wombat (with Bruce Whatley)*
*Pete the Sheep (with Bruce Whatley)*
*Josephine Wants to Dance (with Bruce Whatley)*
*The Shaggy Gully Times (with Bruce Whatley)*
*Emily and the Big Bad Bunyip (with Bruce Whatley)*
*Baby Wombat's Week (with Bruce Whatley)*
*The Tomorrow Book (with Sue deGennaro)*
*Queen Victoria's Underpants (with Bruce Whatley)*
*Christmas Wombat (with Bruce Whatley)*
*A Day to Remember (with Mark Wilson)*
*Queen Victoria's Christmas (with Bruce Whatley)*
*Dinosaurs Love Cheese (with Nina Rycroft)*
*Wombat Goes to School (with Bruce Whatley)*
*The Hairy-Nosed Wombats Find a New Home (with Sue deGennaro)*
*Good Dog Hank (with Nina Rycroft)*
*The Beach They Called Gallipoli (with Bruce Whatley)*
*Wombat Wins (with Bruce Whatley)*

**Jackie French AM** is an award-winning writer, wombat negotiator, the Australian Children's Laureate for 2014–2015 and the 2015 Senior Australian of the Year. She is regarded as one of Australia's most popular children's authors and writes across all genres — from picture books, history, fantasy, ecology and sci-fi to her much loved historical fiction. 'Share a Story' is the primary philosophy behind Jackie's two-year term as Laureate.

jackiefrench.com.au
facebook.com/authorjackiefrench

Jackie French AM is an award-winning writer, wombat negotiator, the Australian Children's Laureate for 2014–2015 and the 2015 Senior Australian of the Year. She is regarded as one of Australia's most popular children's authors and writes across all genres — from picture books, history, fantasy, ecology and sci-fi to her much-loved historical fiction. 'Share a Story' is the primary philosophy behind Jackie's two-year term as Laureate.

jackiefrench.com.au
facebook.com/authorjackiefrench